"I've come to take you back with me!"

Lucien said matter-of-factly as if he was reclaiming something that belonged to him. Troy stepped back instinctively when he came close enough to touch.

"I don't know why you've come all this way simply to start the whole thing again," she told him. Nevertheless the idea of him coming to find her aroused all sorts of infinitely disturbing thoughts, which she did her best to quell before they got out of hand. "The situation hasn't changed with Signora—"

"Have I not told you to leave the matter of the Signora to me?" he demanded.

Troy opened her lips to protest but it was no more than a breath of sound that died when he bent his head and suddenly, quite unexpectedly, pressed his lips to hers.

OTHER
Harlequin Romances
by REBECCA STRATTON

The Corsican Bandit

by

REBECCA STRATTON

Harlequin Books

TORONTO • LONDON • NEW YORK • AMSTERDAM
SYDNEY • HAMBURG • PARIS

Original hardcover edition published in 1978
by Mills & Boon Limited

ISBN 0-373-02222-0

Harlequin edition published December 1978

CHAPTER ONE

THE going was very much harder once she had left the main road, Troy soon discovered, and she rued the fact that her eventual destination lay somewhere up there in the mountain country. The *route nationale* had possessed a good surface and driving had been easy, but once she had taken the turning that brought her .on to the narrow rural road through the hills it seemed that the surface consisted of small boulders.

She told herself repeatedly that it was worthwhile suffering the bumpy, erratic ride, because as it wound its head-spinning way upward and around the lower slopes of the mountain, the road gave breathtaking views of the countryside. The trouble was that she was unable .to enjoy them because there were so many hairpin bends that it was impossible for her to take her eyes from the road for more than a few seconds at a time.

'The scented isle' was one of Corsica's many honorary titles and, even though Troy was prevented by the state of the road from enjoying the scenery as fully as she would have liked, she could at least have the window of the car open and enjoy the deliciously sweet scent of the maquis. The brushwood that covered miles of mountain-side was radiant with spring colours, and it scented the air with a headiness that made it possible to retain her initial sense of anticipation and excitement still.

Then something caught her eye that added a new excitement to her anticipation. A handful of rooftops just glimpsed at above the mass of flowering maquis promised a village just up there on the right, and she instinctively stepped a little more firmly on the acceler-ator. The countryside was undeniably breathtaking, but it somehow seemed also to have a strange sense of emptiness that Troy found overwhelmingly lonely occasionally, and the village, staggering down the sloping hillside, promised human contact.

Troy's idea of visiting Corsica had been partly to see an island that she had been hearing about ever since she was a little girl, from people who knew it well and loved it. It was also partly with the idea of trying to complete her grandfather's book about the wild life of the island, flora and fauna, that she was there. Coming to Corsica had been an impulse, just as so many of her actions were, but it was an impulse that her grandfather Milleaux would have understood. They had been a lot alike, Troy and her grandfather, and she had loved him so dearly that she bit hastily on her lip when she remembered that Grandpère would never be coming back to Corsica again.

Her grandfather's first acquaintance with the island, the mountain in the sea, had been as a young boy, when he had spent several years there with his parents, his father serving as an officer with the French civil administration. Then years later he and his English wife had spent their honeymoon there, and their daughter, who was to become Troy's mother, had often spent holidays there as a child.

But until now Troy had never seen their precious island, their scented isle that they never tired of talking about. It was years now since any of them had been, but her grandfather had never ceased to have a special affection for the place, and his planned book had been as much a labour of love and nostalgia as a serious botanical textbook. It was for that reason that Troy wanted to see it completed.

Troy had always shared her grandfather's interest in wild life, just as she did his sometimes volatile temperament; a temperament that had remained flamboyantly Gallic to the end, no matter how thoroughly anglicised he became in every other way. Her colouring she had inherited from her father's side of the family, and from him she got her thick reddish-brown hair and cornflower blue eyes, but unlike his, her face was small and heart-shaped, fair-skinned and faintly freckled across the bridge of a small straight nose. Her mouth always betrayed her moods, and was full and soft and given to smiling often, just as her mother's was.

She was smiling as she approached another hairpin bend, smiling with anticipation, for once she had negotiated the bend she would find the village that had caught her eye above the profusion of the maquis, and another turn of the wheel proved her right. Tall narrow, multi-storied houses in the Corsican style staggered down the steep hillside on terraced ledges, huddled together instead of spreading out into the vastness of the countryside.

The biggest surprise was to see terrace upon terrace of vines spread out in the sun below the houses, neatly wired and palely green with spring growth against the harsh soil. It was like being whisked suddenly into Italy or France, and it took her completely by surprise, for she had seen so many signs of neglect among the hill villages. There were so many houses left empty, so many groves of almonds and olives left untended and unharvested, that it saddened her. But the signs here were that quite a different situation existed, and she found it encouraging.

Nemio, the village she was in search of, was somewhere on this mountain route, but Troy thought it hardly likely that she had reached it yet, for according to her calculations she had not yet driven far enough. Yet for a moment as she caught sight of it, she wished she had found the village her grandfather had told her of, for somehow this place appealed to her. She had expected almost anything but an obviously flourishing vineyard after the miles of wild scrubland she had driven through, and she was briefly so distracted by what she saw that she was unconscious of anything else.

Driving automatically, she had her eyes on the terraces of vines instead of the road ahead of her, and what happened next happened so quickly and unexpectedly that she had no time to do other than react the way she did. Pressing her foot down hard on the brake was as automatic as twisting the wheel in a desperate attempt to avoid hitting the flying figures that seemed to come out of nowhere and dash wildly in front of her, and she caught her breath in mingled surprise and dismay.

The anticipated bump did not occur and nor did anyone cry out in terror or pain as her car jolted to a halt and threw her forward in her seat, the breath knocked out of her. But it was pure instinct that made her close her eyes tight and sit with her hands holding tightly to the steering wheel, not daring to look.

It was a moment or two before her stunned senses recovered sufficiently for her to realise that the bleating of goats she could hear was in no way a cry of hurt, and the voices of the children were raised in shrill jubilation rather than fear; laughingly scolding rather than frightened, and she took encouragement.

Her last impression, a fleeting one, had been of innumerable goats scampering suddenly from concealment among the maquis, and followed closely by two children, very small children with wildly waving arms. All of them, animals and children, had seemed inevitably destined to finish up under the front wheels of her car, and she could not yet quite believe they hadn't, so she sent up an earnest prayer before she opened her eyes.

It was neither children nor goats who stood looking into the car window, however, but a man who looked perfectly capable of extracting vengeance on behalf of them all, so that Troy caught her breath once more at the sight of him. Heaven knew where he had sprung from, for she had noticed nothing in those few heart-stopping moments but children and goats, but his appearance aroused such vivid memories of the tales of Corsican bandits that her grandfather had regaled her with that Troy stared at him with startled eyes.

She wished she had not been driving with the window down too, for a very large and strong-looking hand had closed itself over the top edge of the door beside her, and looked quite capable of wrenching it from its hinges if the mood took him. Troy was shaking so much with reaction, realising just how close she had come to being involved in a horribly serious accident, that she scarcely realised the man was speaking for a moment, let alone what he was saying.

Fighting against a rising nausea brought on by shock, Troy simply stared at him uncomprehendingly. He was saying something to her in a deep and surprisingly attractive voice, but apart from the fact that she was still dazed, she spoke no Corse and very little French, and she shook her head slowly in bewilderment.

Apparently her lack of response irritated him, for the man leaned down suddenly and a dark frowning face was thrust into the open window, making her draw back hastily. She was overwhelmed by an impression of black eyes, thick black hair and features that were as craggy as the surrounding hills and tanned to a deep brown, and her heart was beating anxiously as she still fought the sickness of shock.

Stunned as she was, she ventured an apology, although she dazedly recognised that she was not altogether to blame, even if she had been momentarily distracted. 'I—I'm very sorry,' she said, and passed the tip of her tongue anxiously across her dry lips, searching hastily for the equivalent French. All Corsicans spoke French, even though their own tongue was used among themselves. '*Je regrette beaucoup.*'

She could only hope he understood she was apologising, for he still looked alarmingly fierce and her

French was very bad. For a second the black eyes seemed to narrow slightly, so that she had a momentary horror of having inadvertently added insult to injury by using wrong words. 'You are English?'

Troy nodded. He still alarmed her, although the fact that he could recognise her nationality and say so in English was some comfort. What she must not do was let him see how nervous he was making her, for his kind of man would probably relish the idea of her being afraid of him.

'Yes, I'm English,' she agreed, and spoke slightly more loudly than usual and with the kind of exaggerated diction that seemed to come naturally when addressing someone not familiar with a language. 'And I really wasn't completely in the wrong, you know. The children——' She stopped there and gave a small sigh of resignation, shaking her head because she suspected his English vocabulary probably consisted of no more than a few stock phrases learned for the benefit of the growing tourist industry. 'Oh, what's the use?' she sighed, as much to herself as to the darkly menacing figure at the window. 'I don't suppose you understand what I'm saying.'

Black brows were arched swiftly, and to her surprise and chagrin laughter glittered for a moment in the black eyes. His teeth gleamed whitely in an alarmingly wolfish smile before he answered her, and he still used English, but with a soft fluid accent that suggested Italian rather than French as his native tongue. His use of the title he called her after a swift check on her naked left hand confirmed her guess.

'On the contrary, *signorina*, I understand perfectly what you are saying!'

Warm colour flooded into Troy's face and she blinked in consternation. If only he was not so close, so able to see and appreciate her embarrassment; but with his face thrust close to hers he was able to judge exactly how discomfited she was by her own *gaffe*, and the black eyes gleamed with what must surely be malicious amusement.

'I didn't realise——' she ventured, but the gaze he fixed on her was relentless as well as disturbing in another way.

It appreciated her discomfiture, but also the small almost childlike features and huge blue eyes; it even swept down as far as the car door allowed and took in the softness of a very feminine figure and a slender waist, and it made Troy more horribly self-conscious than she ever remembered being before. 'Obviously, *signorina*,' he said, and shrugged broad shoulders in acceptance of her unspoken apology.

Seeking a distraction, Troy looked around and noticed that the goats had all disappeared, apparently down the hillside into the all-concealing scrub, but the two children now stood watching with interest from the opposite side of the road, wide dark eyes switching from Troy to the man beside her with undisguised curiosity. They stood silent now, as if their earlier danger was only now brought home to them, and she thought how doll-like and pretty they were.

Presumably the man beside her car was their father, and she could sympathise with their desire to remain at a distance, for he looked as if he would be a stern parent. Indeed she wished she did not feel so alarmingly shaky herself at the thought of his anger, and it was to break the uneasy silence between them that she raised the subject of the children.

'The children weren't hurt at all?' she ventured.

She could see for herself how unharmed they were, but the enquiry served to cover her embarrassment; in fact the children were exhibiting a quite discomfiting amount of interest. But the man apparently took her concern seriously, and he nodded. 'As you can see, *signorina*, they are quite unharmed. But is it not a very dangerous practice to drive an *automobile* with your eyes closed?

Especially on such roads as these.' Troy stared at him uncomprehendingly for a moment, and he went on. 'Are you unwell, perhaps? Your pallor——'

He used his hand to suggest she might have been taken ill, a deception Troy declined to take advantage of. She had, she remembered vaguely, been sitting with her eyes closed when he saw her first, but he surely did not think her such a fool as to have been driving with them closed, even though his words implied it. Another flush, this time one of indignation, coloured her cheeks and her eyes sparkled angrily as she looked into the dark face at the window.

'I wasn't driving with my eyes closed, *monsieur— signore*, or whatever it is I should call you! I'm not a fool and you have no right to suggest I am!' Troy denied it heatedly, but despaired of having stumbled over what to call him. 'I closed my eyes only after I'd taken every precaution. There was nothing I could do but slam on my brakes and try and swerve round them—your chil- dren had no business running into the road as they did, chasing the goats like that! It's a wonder I *didn't* hit one of them, or one of their pets!'

Her anger was such that it did not for the moment occur to her that in an environment like this, goats were far more likely to be a means of livelihood than kept as pets, but it was a slip that the man's expression soon reminded her of. 'The goats belong to someone who keeps them for his living, *signorina*, they are no one's pets, and the children were chasing them from the vines because of the damage they can do. Goats will eat virtu- ally anything,' he added with a look that suggested he hardly expected her to be well enough informed to know that.

Troy resented his manner, she resented his whole atti- tude of superiority, and she was determined to stick to her insistence that she was not the only one at fault for the near accident. 'Nevertheless,' she insisted, 'the children were wrong to run straight out into the road as they did. They could very easily have been killed or at least horribly injured! They should be taught better!'

For a moment she experienced again that alarming nausea when she thought what might have happened, and how the man might have reacted in the event of the children being hurt. His free hand held a long and fairly thick staff almost as high as he was and looked as if it might have been the stripped branch of a tree, and he used it to lean on while he spoke to her, his other hand still resting on the car door.

His hands looked hard and strong and Troy eyed them warily, for she was in pretty wild country here; a country where the vendetta had once been rife. This man looked as if he might still nurture some of the old ways, and Troy hesitated to press her accusations further, even if it meant subduing her own pride.

The soft deep voice scarcely varied its pitch, however, and it sounded no more than gently enquiring, but he hefted the long staff as he spoke and looked across at the children. 'I will see to it that they are suitably punished, if that is what you wish, *signorina*,' he said, and Troy blinked in alarm.

'Oh no, no—I don't want anything like that!'

She glanced hastily at the two children, still standing there beside the road, and felt a twinge of conscience for having blamed them so determinedly. But the small dark faces showed only curiosity and not a trace of apprehension, so probably they had little or no knowledge of English. They also appeared much less upset by their narrow escape than she was herself, but they were no more than six and five years old, she guessed, and Troy felt a tremor of alarm at the idea of them being punished on her word alone.

'They're much too small to realise how dangerous it is for them to go running out into the road as they did,' she insisted. 'The responsibility for their safety rests with the parent who's with them!'

'I agree—*if* he is with them, *signorina*!'

Troy had laid the blame firmly where she saw it due, but he put his argument in the same cool, firm voice he had used all along, and the black eyes showed a hint of malice in their depths, leaving her in no doubt that she had made another mistake. She shook her head in help-less resignation.

'They're not——'

'No, *signorina*, they are not!' He was so obviously relishing the whole wretched situation that Troy felt she could very easily hate the man even if she knew nothing else about him. 'The children are the son and daughter of one of my workers.'

'I'm sorry.'

She should have guessed, Troy told herself, hot with embarrassment because she had made a fool of herself once again. Apart from his impeccable English there were other signs that he was other than a simple son of the soil. His air of arrogance, for one thing, and his boldness in the way he dealt with her; and yet there were things that pointed to him being a manual worker rather than the owner of that vast vineyard up there.

His way of dressing suggested more the man of toil rather than an office man, though there was a pleasantly tangy scent about him that was vaguely familiar as something expensive, as well as the smell of earth and a work-warm body. Serviceable dark cord trousers hugged hips of pantherish leanness, but she told herself she could have noticed that the belt he wore around his lean waist had a buckle of chased silver that was obviously valuable.

A collarless blue and white striped shirt suggested the peasant and had the sleeves rolled up over muscular brown arms, but the addition of a blue and red kerchief knotted around his throat was a theatrical touch that somehow seemed very right on this particular man.

Altogether his appearance gave credence to her first impression of him as the typical Corsican bandit; a relic of the bad old days when fugitives lurked in the forests and mountains of Corsica. A hovering suspicion of that wolfish smile was further cause for uneasiness, but at the same time alarmingly fascinating, she realised.

'You appear to be very shaken by the incident, *signorina*,' he suggested, and Troy noted a little dazedly that he now rested his arm along the roof of her car, the dark face hovering just in sight of the open window, and her voice shivered uncertainly when she hurried recklessly to her own defence.

'Well, naturally I'm shaken—who wouldn't be?'

She had made the admission with no thought of what effect it might have, and she drew back hastily when he put a hand on the handle of the car door with the obvious intention of opening it. 'Then perhaps it would be wiser to take a few moments to recover before you proceed, *signorina*,' he went on. 'If you got out of your car for a few moments, perhaps, and breathed the air deeply, you would feel more—in control; less disturbed.'

'There's really no need for me to get out, thank you!' Troy had a sudden wild urge to restart the engine and get away from there, and she could think of nothing more foolhardy than getting out of her car. With that in mind she held on to the steering-wheel tightly with both hands, as if she feared he might try to pull her from her seat by force. 'I feel much steadier now,' she insisted, 'and I ought to be on my way.'

The man regarded her for a moment, making it plain that he saw right through her bravado, and knew exactly why she was in so much hurry to leave. 'But your hands are trembling, *signorina*, and you should not attempt to drive on such roads as this until you are in full command of yourself.' His voice was quiet but firmly insistent, and Troy suspected he was not in the habit of allowing himself to be persuaded once he had decided.

Then, as if to add pressure to persuasion, he opened the car door and offered her his hand. 'Allow me, *signorina*.'

Suddenly conscious of the fact that her skirt had ridden up while she drove, Troy was aware that far more of her legs was visible than usual, and with one hand she tried to pull it down a little, at least far enough to cover the slim smoothness of limb between thigh and knee. It was not a very successful effort and she was aware that bold black eyes missed nothing, nor were they unappreciative.

'Your hands *are* trembling,' he insisted, soft-voiced, and to give proof to his diagnosis he reached in and covered her hand on the wheel with his. Strong brown fingers enclosed hers completely and exerted just enough pressure to guarantee that if her hands nad not been trembling before, they certainly were now. The craggy face, its mahogany darkness creased with fine lines at the corners of his eyes, leaned closer and Troy caught a glimpse of startlingly white teeth for a moment. 'Be advised, *signorina*, and take time to recover.'

For all its hint of menace, the smile was persuasive, and what he advised was only common sense, Troy recognised. It was much better to take a moment to recover herself than to drive off in her present state of agitation along a road that needed every scrap of anyone's concentration. In the circumstances she complied with his suggestion, although it was evident that she did so only reluctantly, and black brows commented on the fact as she swung her legs round and got out of the car.

The air outside was so much more cool and fresh than in the little car, even with the window opened fully, and the scent of the maquis was headily affecting. Getting out on to the road, however, made Troy realise that her legs were trembling unsteady as well as her hands and, quite instinctively, she clutched at the hand that somehow managed to be in just the right place at the right moment.

Its support steadied her, and looking into the smiling black eyes was unavoidable as he bent his head in solicitous concern over her. For a moment she clung to him, his strong fingers pressing tightly into her hand and the glittering jet-blackness of his eyes enveloping her, then she caught sight of a movement from the corner of her eye, and hastily freed herself, stepping back from him as the children came across the road.

They were enchanting, more so at closer quarters, and they stood with their big dark eyes fixed on her. The idle thought passing into her head, that they could quite easily have belonged to the man beside her, no matter who he was, was hastily dismissed and she bent down to speak to them, smiling automatically. They were irresistible, she thought, and so touchingly solemn.

'Hello.' She ventured thus far and then was not sure how to go on, for children were not within her usual sphere. But a hesitant smile from the boy encouraged her and she pressed on after a second. 'What are your names?' she asked.

The girl was much too shy to answer and turned away with a finger to her mouth, but the boy looked as if he was about to say something when the man took it upon himself to supply her with the information she sought. 'Their names are Jérome and Marie Vincentello, *signorina*,' he told her, 'and they are very sorry to have caused you such distress. Hah?' He looked at the little boy who nodded solemnly in agreement when he repeated the apology in their own tongue. 'They would also like to know your name, *signorina*, naturally.'

Troy knew perfectly well that she was telling him her name because it was he who wanted to know it, but she looked at the two children while she told him. 'My name is Troy Liskard, and I come from Cornwall, in England.'

She clasped the large hand that was thrust towards her automatically. 'I am Lucien Gaffori. You are here on holiday, Signorina Liskard?'

At least he made no pretence that the children had asked about that, and Troy spoke directly to him this time, although it was much more difficult to look at him than she would have believed. Really black eyes, she realised, were disconcertingly hard to meet, especially when they were surrounded by thick lashes that were really quite ridiculously feminine in such a strongly masculine face.

'Actually I'm here to try and finish a book that my grandfather began writing before he died,' Troy said, and wondered fleetingly why on earth she was standing here on a wild mountain road talking to a complete stranger about her grandfather. 'It's all about the wild life of Corsica.'

'Ah!' Interest gleamed in his eyes and it was clear that he would like to hear more about her project. 'Your grandfather was Corsican, perhaps, *signorina*?'

'He was French, actually,' Troy told him, 'but he spent a lot of his childhood here, and he always loved Corsica.'

Briefly that somewhat wolfish smile showed again and he nodded. 'He was a very wise man, *signorina*!'

Since he seemed interested there was no reason why she should not take advantage of the fact and seek his help in finding Nemio, the village her grandfather had liked so much, and she looked at him enquiringly. 'I'm looking for a village called Nemio,' she said. 'I know it's on this route somewhere, but I'm not quite sure how much further I have to go. Could you give me some idea——'

'You need look no further, *signorina*!' A big hand spread extravagantly to take in the surrounding country-side as well as the jumble of stone houses. 'You are most welcome to Nemio!'

Troy's laughter was instinctive and she had no idea just how much it did for her small face and big corn-flower blue eyes. 'Do you mean I've arrived without knowing it?' she asked, and Lucien Gaffori smiled.

He appreciated the effect of her laughter and it showed in his eyes as he nodded agreement. 'You have indeed, Signorina Liskard. Do you have friends here, perhaps?'

Something in his voice gave a moment's uneasiness, and Troy looked up at him for a second before she answered. 'My grandfather knew some people here many years ago,' she told him. 'It's a name I've often heard him mention, though it's a long time since he was in touch last. The Ciari family; do you know them? Mr Sampiero Ciari in particular, he and my grandfather got along well when he and my grandmother stayed here last. Whenever he stayed in Nemio, the Ciaris always put him up.'

It was obvious that he was going to disappoint her, she had anticipated it from the moment he asked if she had friends there, and the chill of disillusion already overlaid her initial excitement. 'Alas, *signorina*,' he told her, apparently with genuine regret, 'the Ciari family are no longer here. The old people, the ones your grandfather would have known, died some years ago, I believe, and the sons——' He shrugged, accepting with regret, as so many did, that far too many of Corsica's young people left their homeland each year in search of a better living standard. 'The house is empty, crumbling, like so many others.'

All too often Troy had come across the same story as she came through country villages on her way, and it was possible, if you looked more closely than she had until now, to see that several of the houses that came striding down the steep hillside were no longer inhabited or habitable. The place had slightly less of an air of neglect than many of those she had seen, mostly because of that thriving vineyard, but it was a sad fact, she realised, that the countryside was slowly losing its life either to other European countries or to the more salubrious tourist spots near the coast. Apparently her grandfather's old friends had joined the exodus to richer pastures.

'I see.'

At this point Troy was unsure what to do next. Rather rashly she had depended upon the Ciaris being able to find room for her on the spur of the moment as they had sometimes done for her grandfather, but she could see with the wisdom of hindsight that she should have checked with them first. There were other places, of course, equally suited to her purpose, but she had set her heart on Nemio, and she was not easily turned from an idea once she had settled on it.

For the moment she had completely forgotten where she was and that the man and two small children still watched her with polite curiosity and possibly with sympathy too. It was a moment or two before she recovered sufficiently to realise that if anyone could help her to realise her original ambition to stay in Nemio it was the man who now waited patiently to see what she was going to do.

'I am sorry to be the bearer of unhappy news, *signorina*.' The deep quiet voice broke into her thoughts and Troy took a moment to regard him from the concealment of her lashes. 'You were perhaps expecting the Ciaris to—house you?' he suggested, and Troy admitted it with a resigned shrug.

'I was, but I don't imagine it's very easy finding accommodation right out here in the wilds, is it? I'll have to drive back to the nearest town and try there.'

There was amusement as well as speculation in the black eyes as they regarded her steadily for a moment before he answered. 'Do you particularly wish to be accommodated in the wilds, *signorina*?' The children stood either side of him, curious and wondering perhaps why he did not simply see the foreign woman on her way and take them back home. Similar thoughts were crossing Troy's mind too, but apparently he was interested enough to remain and she had a vague hope that he might yet solve her problem of where to stay. 'It is possible that I can assist your search, if you wish to stay in Nemio,' he said, and Troy's heart gave a great leap of anticipation as she looked up at him hopefully.

'Could you?' she asked, then glanced at the tiers of grapevines that covered the hillside in the warm spring sunshine. 'I'd be most grateful if you could find me somewhere. I didn't realise you took in visitors as well as grew grapes!'

A ghost of a smile hovered for a moment around his mouth and made her suspect that she had said the wrong thing yet again. 'I do not normally—take in visitors, as you say, *signorina*, but in this instance I am sure that a place can be found for you. Most of the people of Nemio work for me, but there is no one with room for an extra one. Big families, you understand,' he added with a flash of that wolfish smile. 'If you will accept my hospitality, you will be welcome.'

It was more than she expected, and a little disturbing to think of him as her landlord for the next few weeks, so that she hesitated without being aware of it until a black brow twitched in question and had her hastily seeking a reply. 'That's very kind of you, Signor Gaffori, if you're sure your wife won't mind.'

'It is unlikely, *signorina*,' he informed her with a solemnity that was belied by the gleaming laughter in his eyes. 'I am unmarried! But I have a *massaia*, a—how is it?—a housekeeper.'

'Oh, I see. I'm sorry, I——'

'Assumed that I should have a wife?' he asked, mockery in the soft, deep voice, and once more strong teeth showed in a smile that could not fail to make her uneasy. 'I manage well enough without one, *signorina*!'

Troy had no difficulty believing it, and she vaguely wondered how many eligible young women there were in a village the size of Nemio. 'Perhaps,' she ventured, 'I could find someone who puts up visitors—I mean someone who would be glad to make a little extra for a few weeks.'

Her meaning was unmistakable, but the man seemed to accept her misgivings without rancour and the black eyes gleamed with laughter as he looked down at her from his superior height. 'There is no need for you to fear for your honour, *signorina*, if that is what troubles you! Close by my home there is a small *casetta* that I think will suit you well for a few weeks, and you will have to answer to no one since it is quite separate.'

'A cottage?' That was different altogether, and Troy's heart took courage again. 'That sounds wonderful—I could be quite independent and not trouble anyone, if you're sure you don't mind.'

A hint of a bow dismissed any suggestion of his minding, and he brought his face down nearer to hers as he pointed along the steep upward climb of the road. 'If you continue along this way, you will see very shortly a turning that appears to go into a field, but if you follow it it will lead you past one or two smaller houses to my home. A little beyond this you will find the *casetta* I have told you of; my housekeeper has the key. Madame Coron; if you say that I have sent you, she will make you welcome!'

'Thank you, I'm very grateful.' It was unbelievable luck, and as yet Troy found it hard to believe it had happened to her. 'I'll go right there now, if that's all right.'

'It is perfectly all right, *signorina*.' He inclined his head in a brief bow, then bent and took the children by the hand, looking up again with a smile. 'I wonder if in return you would do something for me, Signorina Liskard? Would you be so kind as to return the children to their home? It is upon your way.'

'Oh yes, of course!'

She had no objection at all to having the two mites

with her while she drove in search of her cottage in the mountains—they would perhaps serve to keep her mind off the fact that she was going to be in pretty close proximity for the next few weeks to the most disturbing man she had ever met. He saw her into her car again, then put the two children into the back seat, and they tumbled in, chattering together and laughing, obviously thrilled at getting an unexpected ride home.

Lucien Gaffori closed the door on them very carefully, then came around to the driver's seat once more, resting his hand on the door as he had before, and regarding Troy with a steadiness that she found horribly disconcerting in the circumstances. She was only thankful that he had not begged a lift home for himself too.

'I will see you very soon, Signorina Liskard,' he told her. 'Meanwhile you will find my *massaia* very helpful, I am certain. She will see that you have everything that you need. She speaks some English.'

'Well, that's a relief anyway!' She laughed at her own shortcomings as a linguist, then hastily started up the engine when she saw the man's black eyes respond to her laughter. 'Thank you once again, Signor Gaffori; I'll see you later.'

'*Ciao!*'

With the children waving enthusiastically from the rear window Troy started once more up the steep mountain road with a tingle of irresistible excitement stirring her blood, and smiling to herself when she thought how differently the encounter with Lucien Gaffori could have ended. With a small cottage available for her, her problem was solved and she could settle down to several weeks of uninterrupted work on her grandfather's book.

The vineyards seemed endless and by the time Troy found the turning he had told her about, she began to wonder just how big a man Lucien Gaffori was. Obviously he had not been merely making an idle boast when he claimed the children's father worked for him, for a

board set slightly askew in the corner of a field proclaimed it as belonging to L. Gaffori and gave the name
as La Casa Antica.

There were one or two small houses up ahead, and
also some obviously new buildings that looked as if they
might be storage sheds or places for making wine—Troy
was abysmally ignorant of such matters, though she
hated to admit it. At the other end of the track road she
could see a large white house, perched at the top of a
steep slope, but she had little opportunity to look too far
ahead as the way was rutted with tractor tracks and she
needed all her concentration to keep her little car on the
straight course. Some of the profits Lucien Gaffori must
make from such an enterprise, she thought wryly, could
well be spent on resurfacing the roads.

'Mademoiselle! C'est ça, c'est ça!' The little boy was
standing immediately behind her and pointing out a
small stone cottage that stood close beside the track, and
Troy turned hastily while his voice shrilled in her ear
still. 'Arrêtez-vous ici, mademoiselle!'

Giving him a smile over her shoulder, Troy braked to
a halt, then got out to open the door for them. 'This is
where you live?' They might not understand what she
was saying, but the smile would encourage them, and
they were both smiling a little shyly as they clambered
out of the back seat. 'Perhaps I'll see you again,' she
ventured, and the boy gave her a solemn and rather
touching little bow.

'Merci, mademoiselle.' He was so sweet and old-
fashioned that Troy's impulsive reaction was to hug him,
but she recalled herself in time and realised he would
probably find the gesture more embarrassing than gratifying. 'Au revoir, mademoiselle!'

'Au revoir, Jerome; Marie!'

If she was going to be around for several weeks she
was quite likely to bump into them again, and she might
as well make friends from the outset. They waved her off

as she drove on up towards the big white house at the top of the slope, and being alone once more Troy felt a kind of apprehensive excitement at what lay before her.

The house looked new now that she could see it more clearly, but it blended in well with the wild landscape and looked as if it might have grown from the mountainside just as the others did, except that it was a dazzling white instead of a natural stone colour like them. It was surrounded by outbuildings of various sizes, but she could see nothing that resembled a cottage.

A drive of sorts curved around in front of it and gave plenty of room for parking on a wide stony square in front of the house. She had scarcely stopped the car's engine when the door opened and a tall black-haired woman came out, standing first for a few moments on the top step before coming down to meet her as she got out of the car. Her expression was neither discouraging nor welcoming, but more curious than anything else, and Troy assumed she was Lucien Gaffori's housekeeper.

Hastily she recalled the name he had used and smiled as she spoke. 'Madame Coron?'

The woman nodded, her curiosity increasing if the look in her bright dark eyes was any guide. 'Oui, mademoiselle—qu'y a-t'il pour votre service?'

She had been told that the woman spoke English, a little English, according to her employer, and Troy wondered how little as she smiled apologetically and spread her hands. 'I'm afraid my French is very poor,' she told her, 'but Monsieur—Signor Gaffori says you speak a little English.'

Troy's heart sank when the woman made a grimace and spread her hands in a copy of her own gesture of regret. 'A little only, mademoiselle, je regrette.'

It was going to be hard, but Troy smiled determinedly and used her hands a lot in the hope that she could somehow convey what she meant without giving this rather solemn-looking woman the wrong impression of her meeting with Lucien Gaffori. 'Monsieur—Signor Gaffori said there was a cottage here somewhere, that I could use.'

'Monsieur Gaffori is a—friend of *mademoiselle*? Ah, *mais oui*, now I have the understanding!' She unhesitatingly used the French title, not the Italian as Troy had done, but it was a small enough difference, at least they had the same man in mind. The woman glanced in at the suitcases tucked down between the front and back seats. '*Votre bagage?*'

Following her meaning, Troy nodded. 'Oh yes, my luggage, but it doesn't want to be taken out of the car now, does it?' Obviously she was not making herself clear and she shook her head, searching for the French word for cottage and failing to come up with it. Perhaps if she told her room and then worked from there it might be easier. '*Une chambre*, Monsieur Gaffori said——'

'Ah, *mais oui!*' Apparently she had made herself understood, for the woman was smiling and nodding. '*Oui, mademoiselle, je comprends!*'

Pursing her lips in a silent whistle of relief, Troy smiled. 'Thank goodness!' she said, and looked beyond the housekeeper to where a short and very stout man was coming around the corner of the house.

Obviously a workman of some kind, he changed direction when Madame Coron called him over, but the housekeeper apparently had not the patience to wait for him to arrive, and she walked towards him, indicating by signs that Troy should come too. They met half way across the stony square and at once the two indulged in a loud and garrulous exchange which filled Troy with curiosity.

The man eyed her with what she could only describe as a leer, and was soundly berated for it, if she judged the woman's reactions correctly. Then she indicated the car containing her suitcases and gave a shrug of resignation as she smiled once more at Troy. 'François will attend to your *bagage, mademoiselle*. You will take *café, oui*?'

Supposing her suitcases were to be taken to her cottage, wherever it might be, Troy nodded gratefully. Coffee would be welcome, the last hour or so had been rather a trial one way and the other, and Madame Coron seemed friendly enough now that they had established a form of communication.

'I'd love some coffee, thank you,' she told her, and followed her into the house. Glancing over her shoulder, she saw that the man's eyes still followed her, and he was still leering, although he turned away when she caught his eye, and opened the car door to take out her suitcases. No doubt he would find her somewhere to park her car too, later on when she had had her coffee. Things were turning out rather better than she expected.

CHAPTER TWO

APPARENTLY Madame Coron had decided that Troy
should be treated as an honoured guest and, having
heard of the warmth of Corsican hospitality from her
grandfather, she was delighted to be the recipient of it.
She was shown into a big, bright room, warm with
spring sunshine and quite staggeringly luxurious when
she considered the wildness of the countryside surrounding the house.

The comparative newness of the building itself was
not too apparent because the grace of antiquity had been
so skilfully reproduced, and Troy suspected that the
furniture in the room was genuinely old and must have
been worth a small fortune. Obviously Lucien Gaffori
did not believe in stinting himself.

The coffee she had been promised on arrival was
quickly forthcoming, and served to her in fine bone
china on a silver tray. During the first few moments
Troy felt a little uncomfortable when she thought of his
reaction if he returned and found her there, drinking
coffee in his elegant *salon* as if she was an invited guest,
but her pleasure after the first few moments banished
any serious concern about it.

Maybe she should have told Madame Coron that she
preferred to go directly to her borrowed cottage instead
of succumbing to the temptation of coffee after her journey, but in fact she had expected to be having it in the
kitchen as the guest of the housekeeper instead of finding
herself in sole possession of this big, luxurious room.
The initial surprise had been the reason she simply
accepted the situation without comment.

Also she was curious, she readily admitted it. She

wanted to see what sort of things a man like Lucien
Gaffori surrounded himself with in his own home, and
now she knew. He had impeccable taste and he was
extravagant. He must also be ungrudging of hospitality,
or he would not have offered her the use of the cottage,
so she had no reason to suppose he would object to her
being given coffee, and with that comforting thought she
consoled herself.

Since she had the opportunity to take stock of her
surroundings, uninhibited by the company of her host,
Troy did so with interest, and she liked what she saw.
Quite a few of the paintings that hung on the pale yellow
walls were originals, she guessed, and she was sufficiently well informed in her modest way to recognise the
artists. Works by two of the earlier French Impression-
ists shared space with an exquisite Renaissance Mad-
onna and Child that was so lushly Italian that she felt
sure it must be a favourite with her host, especially since
it was hung to its best advantage, where the light
brought out the glowing colours.

There was a great deal of gilt decorating walls and
ceiling that reminded her of Roman *palazzi* more than a
Corsican farmer's house, and elegant mirrors reflected a
mass of *objets d'art* covering a variety of periods, so that
Troy wondered if it reflected only one man's taste or
several. But it was a comfortable room for all its gran-
deur and it struck Troy suddenly how much at home she
felt there; which in view of her initial encounter with its
owner was quite surprising.

Where she sat, in one of the slender-legged armchairs
upholstered in yellow brocade, the sun was warm and
she felt pleasantly relaxed as she started to pour herself
a second cup of coffee. A second later she almost dropped the delicate china pot on to the tray when the door
of the *salon* opened and her host walked in. He regis-
tered no surprise at the sight of her, so Troy assumed he
had already spoken with his housekeeper, but a dis-

concerting hint of amusement hovered about the wide sensual mouth and made her uneasy.

Putting down the coffee pot with studied care, she got to her feet instinctively, smoothing down the skirt of her dress in an unconscious gesture of nervousness as he came across the room to her, and not quite sure what to say. In the event, he saved her the trouble of having to say anything, for he came and sat himself in another chair, after indicating that she should resume her own seat, and picked up the coffee pot.

He gave it an experimental shake to satisfy himself that there was still something left in it, then looked across at her and smiled. 'I am pleased that you found your way here, *signorina*,' he said, and went on before Troy had time to recover sufficiently to reply. 'I have asked Madame Coron to bring me another cup; you will stay and drink a second cup of coffee with me, will you not?'

'I was just——' Troy started to say that she had been on the point of leaving, but obviously he had noticed her in the act of replenishing her cup when he came in.

'Oh, but of course, you were already pouring yourself another cup when I came in,' he said with a light shrug by way of an apology. 'Please allow me, *signorina*!'

He leaned forward in his chair and refilled her cup, pushing it back towards her, and Troy kept her hands folded together in her lap, trying to control their persistent unsteadiness. He was, she realised, no less disconcerting here in this elegant *salon* that he had been out there on the mountain road.

'That's very kind of you, thank you. I wasn't expecting to be given coffee,' she explained with a curiously shaky little laugh. 'I hope your housekeeper wasn't taking too much on herself by bringing it for me; she was, as you said, very welcoming.'

'But of course!' Madame Coron came in with another cup and saucer for him which he took with a word of thanks and a slight nod that indicated she should leave them again. Troy barely glanced at her, but during the few seconds when she did, she noticed a curiously speculative look on the woman's face before she withdrew as she was bid. 'Until you have purchased supplies for yourself, *signorina*,' Lucien Gaffori went on, 'you cannot be allowed to go without food and drink, and I have no doubt that a cup of coffee was welcome after such a journey.'

'Oh, indeed it was!' The need to do her own catering if she rented a cottage instead of stayed in someone's home had not occurred to her until now, and Troy was not devious enough to conceal the fact from him. He was smiling, she noticed, when she stared at him somewhat vaguely. 'I wasn't expecting to have to cater for myself when I came,' she confessed. 'I was banking on the Ciaris putting me up as they used to my grandfather; I imagine it means a drive into the nearest town to get what I want, doesn't it?'

'It will be necessary,' Lucien Gaffori agreed as he sipped his coffee, 'but meanwhile you may borrow anything that you require from Madame Coron. Please,' he hastened to add when she looked like arguing the point, 'there is no need to concern yourself, Signorina Liskard. It is some distance to drive when stocks need replenishing and we have a well stocked store cupboard, you will find; have no fear that you will inconvenience me at all.'

This was the very best in hospitality, Troy thought, and relaxed just a little more as she drank her second cup of coffee. The fates certainly seemed to be smiling on her at the moment. 'I'm very grateful,' she told him with a smile that gave warmth to her blue eyes and found a fleeting dimple at one corner of her mouth. 'You've been very good—letting me have the cottage, giving me coffee and now offering me supplies until I can do some shopping. I really am grateful and I *will* borrow from your store cupboard, as you suggest, then replace whatever I take when I go shopping. Thank you.'

'*Prego, signorina!*'

Once more that gleaming smile caused a shiver of sensation to flutter along her spine, but Troy hastily dismissed it as a relic of childhood imagination. By telling her such vivid tales of Corsica's more lurid past, her grandfather had influenced her first impression of this tall, dark man she had come upon with such startling unexpectedness on a mountain road. But Lucien Gaffori was a polite and sophisticated European, not a mountain brigand, no matter how closely he resembled the popular conception of one, and she was grateful for his hospitality.

After a surreptitious look at him over the rim of her cup, she ventured a smile. 'I've been very lucky in Corsica so far,' she told him. 'I never dreamed I'd be fortunate enough to find a cottage to rent; in fact I still find it hard to believe that it's happened!'

Black eyes held hers steadily for a moment, and something gleamed in their depths that gave her a moment of uncertainty, so that she took a sip of coffee by way of a distraction. 'You told Madame Coron that I had given permission for you to use the *casetta*—the cottage, *signorina*?'

'Yes.' Troy put down her cup carefully on to the tray, and looked across at him, unable to disguise the wariness she felt suddenly. 'I had a bit of difficulty making her understand what I was talking about at first, but she understood eventually.'

'What exactly was it that you told her, *signorina*?'

Sensing a trap, Troy was still wary, but his voice was pitched low and had a smooth silkiness that slid along her spine and made her shiver involuntarily, and she shook her head without really knowing why she did it. 'I don't quite understand you,' she told him. 'I simply told her what you said—that I could use the cottage.'

'I think not *exactly* so, eh?'

Troy blinked anxiously and her hands were clasped tightly together on her lap. 'Well, actually,' she explained reluctantly, 'I couldn't think of the French for cottage——'

'*Chaumière*, Signorina Liskard; the word is *chaumière*!'

Troy frowned in sudden irritation over his splitting hairs. Madame Coron had understood her eventually, and it seemed a little pernickety of him to point out her lack of knowledge quite so insistently. 'Yes, of course, I remember it now, but at the time I couldn't think of it, so I used *chambre* to convey what I meant. I know that means room and not cottage,' she hastened to add when he showed signs of pointing out her error, 'but it didn't matter, surely, since Madame Coron got the message!'

In his big hands the fragile china cup and saucer looked in danger of being crushed, but he handled them with infinite care as he drained the contents, then put them down on the tray, and his eyes gleamed at her darkly from their thick fringe of lashes. 'It would appear not so, *mia cara signorina*,' he said in a voice that was threaded through with laughter. 'Madame Coron got a quite different message from the one you intended—at least, I assume that she did. Your *bagage* was placed in my bedroom!'

Troy felt the colour flood into her face, and she had a sudden insane desire to get up and run out of the room and hide somewhere. No wonder Madame Coron had looked at her so curiously when she came into the room just now. She could see how it had happened. Her use of the word *chambre* immediately followed by his name had seemed to bring enlightenment to the woman, but Troy could see now how she had misled her. The possibility of Lucien Gaffori thinking she had deliberately misled his housekeeper did not bear thinking about, and she clasped her hands together tightly, unable to meet his eyes.

'I can't imagine—I just can't imagine how such a mistake can have happened,' she said, feigning ignorance for the moment and wishing her voice was not quite so unsteady. 'I just don't know.' She shook her head vaguely and firmly controlled the desire to get up and go. 'I'm very sorry.'

'There is no need, *signorina*,' he insisted. 'I am flattered!'

Troy looked up, her eyes huge and anxious, blaming him for making an already embarrassing situation even more discomfiting. 'You can't think I *meant* that to happen!' she declared, her voice husky. 'You can't possibly! You must know——'

A large hand, turned palm towards her, waved slowly back and forth to reassure her. 'I was as puzzled as you were yourself initially, *signorina*,' he told her. 'It was your use of the word *chambre*——' He shrugged with the explicitness that only a Latin could get into the gesture, and Troy got hastily to her feet.

For a moment she stood looking down at him, but then he too stood up, facing her across the low table that held the coffee tray. 'I think the best thing for me to do is to be on my way, Monsieur—Signor Gaffori,' she said, huskily breathless. 'If you'll please get someone to get my cases back——'

'Ah, *signorina*!'

'That man—the one your housekeeper called over to take my cases out to the car, do you think I can face him again knowing that he thought——' She recalled the swarthy face and its unmistakable leer and shook her head quickly at what she now knew must have been going on behind that leer. 'Oh, for heaven's sake, please get him to bring my luggage down again and put it in my car, then I'll go!'

'But why so, *signorina*?'

'You must know why so!' she gasped, but felt a twinge of regret for her plans nevertheless. It had all seemed to be working so perfectly.

But he was shaking his head, apparently surprised that she was taking it all so seriously, and Troy half-wished she could accept it as matter-of-factly as he did. She had made so many embarrassing mistakes since their first dramatic encounter, and she felt that the longer she stayed around him the worse things would get. There were other villages where she could stay that did not have such distractions as Lucien Gaffori—but still in her heart she wanted to stay in Nemio, as Grandpère had, and the wish was the reason she sought a way out.

'I seem to keep putting my foot in it,' she told him, and saw the way he frowned over an apparently unfamiliar saying. 'I mean I——'

'I believe I know your meaning, *signorina*,' he said, and spoke for the moment with no sign of facetiousness. 'But surely the fact that my *massaia* misunderstood you is no reason to abandon what is a perfectly good arrangement. You have spoken yourself of how pleased you are to have the use of the *casetta*; why should you now decide differently because of a foolish mistake; a misunderstanding of little consequence?'

He was right, of course, she recognised it in her own mind. But *he* was not constantly recalling the face of the man who had carried her suitcases up to Lucien Gaffori's bedroom. 'I can't forget the way that awful man leered——'

'François would have leered had you been twice your age and as ugly as the very devil,' Lucien Gaffori assured her, and once more she had to admit that he was probably right. He had moved closer without her noticing and when Troy looked up and found him standing directly in front of her, near enough for her to be affected by the disturbing aura of maleness that surrounded him, she caught her breath. 'I have already instructed him to transfer your *baggage* to the cottage,' he said. 'Is it not unreasonable for you to change your mind? Both François and Madame Coron are in no doubt of your true position, Signorina Liskard. I have made it clear that a mistake was made and I am sure that Madame Coron will tender her apologies for your embarrassment, given the opportunity.'

'But *you* found it amusing!' The accusation was irresistible as a last stand, whether or not he attempted to deny it.

As it happened he did not. 'The situation seemed to me to have an element of the French farce, and I confess I was amused by it, but I am sorry that you were embarrassed, *signorina*.' He spoke quietly and apparently seriously, but when she looked up swiftly to deny that she saw any humour in the situation, Troy caught a lurking gleam of laughter in the black eyes and hastily looked away. 'I had thought the English possessed of a sense of humour, but I am sorry if I was mistaken,' he added, and thus issued a challenge that was hard to resist.

'Nobody enjoys looking a fool,' Troy objected, wishing that gleam of laughter was not so dangerously infectious. 'Even if my own actions did contribute to it.'

'Not foolish, *signorina*, merely—unfortunate in your choice of a word.' He stood for a moment just studying her, as if he might be trying to anticipate her answer. 'How shall I instruct François?' he asked.

Troy kept her eyes averted because she did not want to see his reaction, whatever it was, when she gave in. 'It *is* very convenient,' she allowed, 'so I'll take the cottage, if you're still agreeable—thank you.'

'*Bene!*' He voiced his approval softly, but with such obvious satisfaction that just for a moment Troy felt a twinge of misgiving once more. 'I will show you to the cottage myself, *signorina*. Please come with me.'

The cottage was nearer to the house than she expected, with merely a stretch of stony ground between the two buildings, similar to that in the front of the house, where her car was parked, and Troy felt the ir-

repressible tingle of excitement stirring in her once more
as she walked beside Lucien Gaffori. She was not quite
sure what she had expected it to be like, but certainly
nothing like it was.

In the circumstances she was not surprised to find it a
rough and ready stone house with a heavy slate roof and
narrow windows. She would not have been surprised to
discover that it was one of those abandoned, as so many
were, or perhaps simply temporarily vacated by one of
the estate workers and awaiting a new tenant. The outward appearance confirmed her expectations, but having
set foot inside she was obliged to think again, for obviously no field worker had lived there.

It was tall and narrow with three stories, built upward
rather than outward as most of them were, but there the
resemblance ended, for it was as extravagantly furnished and decorated as the main house, but on a smaller
scale. The small *salon* was richly carpeted and furnished
with similar chairs to those in the bigger house, and
there were two bedrooms, both furbished with the same
extravagant taste.

A bathroom was installed on the third floor, and gave
dizzying views of mountain pastures and thick acres of
maquis, blazingly colourful in the spring sunshine that
warmed the scents of myrtle, honeysuckle and wild mint
and filled the air with them. No scented bath-salts could
ever have competed with them.

From the bedroom windows it was possible to make
out a complicated system of irrigation, weaving its way
among the terraces of vines and seemingly drawn from a
gleaming ribbon of water higher up in the mountain. The
same source probably provided the domestic supply too,
and Troy marvelled at the amount of planning that must
have gone into creating this oasis of luxury, as well as
the cost. Altogether the place delighted her, and she did
not hesitate to say so.

'It's wonderful,' she declared for the umpteenth time

as she walked down the narrow staircase behind her host, and Lucien Gaffori turned and smiled at her lazily over his shoulder. 'It's so different from what I was expecting; I never dreamed there was anything like this out here in——'

'In the wilds?' Lucien Gaffori drawled, and reminded her that those were her own words when she spoke of the surrounding countryside earlier. But he laughed and gave her no time to say anything, settling himself on the ledge of the *salon* window that overlooked the sweeping, vine-covered terraces. 'I am pleased that you like it, *signorina*,' he said.

Feeling delighted with her surprise, Troy smiled. 'It *is* a surprise, finding all this—luxury in what looks from outside like a perfectly ordinary little house.'

'It was once a very ordinary little house, as you say,' he told her, glancing out of the window. 'Now it is used by my two nephews when they visit me from Italy. It was necessary to house them—in the style to which they are accustomed.' He added the cliché with a touch of irony that Troy noted.

'I see.'

In her opinion that big house should have been amply large enough to house a quite big family and she would probably have said so, but Lucien Gaffori seemed to have the uncanny and rather disconcerting knack of following her train of thought. Smiling as he explained, he used his big hands to lend explicit meaning to what he was saying.

'It is more—free, for them, you understand,' he said, and a gleam in his black eyes suggested that his nephews had something of their uncle in their make-up. The fact that he was laughing lent strength to the suspicion. 'My sister and her husband and the little girls sleep in the main house,' he went on, 'but it suits the two boys much better to use the cottage. They are older, you understand; sixteen and seventeen years; young men, with the need to—do things that young men do.'

'I understand perfectly,' Troy told him, and perhaps gave the slightest edge to the words without being aware of it.

The black eyes gleamed at her, bright with meaning, and she felt a momentary warmth in her cheeks as she hastily avoided looking at him. 'I am sure that you do, *signorina*!'

'Your nephews don't sound so very different from my cousins,' she said, 'though they don't get quite so much encouragement from their uncles.'

Heavy lashes half-concealed the gleaming eyes and his mouth smiled, vaguely mocking. 'You disapprove of my—encouraging my sister's sons, *signorina*?'

'Certainly not!' Troy denied hastily. 'It isn't my place to disapprove of anything you choose to do, Signor—Monsieur Gaffori!' Once more she wished she did not so often stumble over what to call him. Madame Coron used Monsieur, yet somehow he seemed so very Italian that Troy found it almost automatic to call him Signor. 'I'm sorry,' she said, bringing her confusion into the open. 'I'm never quite sure what I should call you—Signor Gaffori, or Monsieur Gaffori, as Madame Coron does.'

He regarded her for a moment in silence, the black eyes almost slumbrous between their thick lashes, then he crossed his arms over his chest and leaned back comfortably against the window frame. 'If you find it confusing, *mia cara signorina*,' he said, 'please call me Lucien; I have no objection whatever!'

Taken by surprise, Troy carefully avoided looking at the slight smile that hovered about his mouth. 'You *are* Italian, aren't you?' she asked, ignoring the invitation for the moment, and he arched one black brow at her obvious evasion.

'I am Italian born, *signorina*,' he told her. 'My mother is Italian, but my father is Corsican, he was born here, in

Nemio—in this very house.'

'In *this* house?' Troy looked around the little *salon*, and guessed it had not looked as it did now when Lucien Gaffori's father lived there.

'That is right,' he confirmed. 'Although it was not as you see it now. My grandfather was a shepherd, just as my father was until he left to find greener pastures.'

'Like so many do,' Troy nodded understandingly.

'As you say. In Italy my father learned how to grow the grapes for wine and he worked so hard and became so skilled that he not only eventually married his employer's daughter, but also became a very wealthy man in his own right. It was quite an achievement for a Corsican shepherd boy, you will grant, *signorina*.' He spoke with pride and no trace of regret for his humble origins, and Troy was touched to realise the obviously deep love he had for his father. 'When I came here,' he went on, 'I named this whole estate for this one little house where he was born. La Casa Antica—the old house.'

'Oh yes, of course.'

A quizzical smile questioned her response. 'You speak some Italian, Signorina Liskard?'

Shaking her head, Troy confessed her shortcomings on the question of languages other than her own. 'I'm afraid I don't speak anything but English,' she confessed, 'although I often wish I did.'

'Not even French!' She found it hard to forgive him that sly dig at her unfortunate mistake over the cottage, but decided to ignore it.

'Not enough to carry on a conversation,' she admitted, and noted that he seemed in no hurry to leave, so that she wondered if he ever did anything more than oversee the vast acreage of vines he owned, for all he dressed like a field worker.

'You told me that your grandfather was French, did you not?' he asked, and Troy nodded.

'My mother's father was French,' she agreed, 'but he spoke English without a trace of accent, and he seldom spoke French at all after he married my grandmother, I believe. He spoke only English when I knew him.'

'A pity,' he observed frankly. 'My father has always spoken to me in French and also in Corse, his native *patois*, and my mother speaks to me in Italian. I was perhaps fortunate that I was able to learn all three from the beginning.'

'You also speak very good English,' Troy said unhesitatingly, then hastily avoided the smile that thanked her for the compliment, because she found it oddly disturbing.

'I have known several English people during the past few years,' he explained, 'some of them quite—intimately.' She was left to draw her own conclusions from that, while he went on to another subject altogether. 'Is it not possible,' he suggested, 'that my father may recollect having seen or even spoken to your grandfather? Papa also knew the old Ciaris, and he would be much the same age as your grandfather, I think.'

'Oh, I hardly think so!' Troy denied it before she stopped to think that it might just be possible. 'Grand-père was seventy-four when he died last year.'

'And my papa is seventy-three years! Fortunes are long in making, *signorina*,' he added with a wry smile. 'Also one must take into account the fact that I am——' he spread his hands expressively and smiled, 'at least a few years older than you are, and that I have an older sister. It is quite possible, you see, *mia cara signorina*!'

'Yes. Yes, I can see it could be.' He was about twelve or thirteen years her senior, Troy guessed, and if he had an older sister—— Somehow the conversation had taken on a disturbingly personal character and she found it hard to bring herself back to more commonplace matters, much as she felt she ought to. 'You're not expecting your nephews to stay, are you?' she asked, firmly dismissing comparisons. 'I don't like to think of them having to stay close under the parental eye because I have their cottage.'

'Please do not concern yourself, *signorina*,' he begged as he heaved himself away from the supporting window frame. Standing tall and somehow menacing in the small room, he looked down at her. 'The summer *vacanza* does not begin yet and they are both still at school!'

'Oh, good!' It was maddening to feel so nervous of him when in fact he had done nothing to give cause for complaint. The fact that he aroused curious and disturbing responses in her that she could neither explain nor control was not something she could blame him for, and she did her best to sound cool and matter-of-fact. 'I think I'm going to like it here,' she decided, putting more distance between them without making it too obvious. 'Once I've put my things away, and settled down to work on the book, I shall feel quite at home.'

He was watching her as she moved away and she hoped he was not aware that he was the cause of her restlessness. 'I am pleased to hear you say so,' he told her, and thrusting his hands into the pockets of the dark trousers he continued to watch her for a second or two before moving in the direction of the door. Instead of keeping going, however, he paused beside her and his proximity once more alerted her senses. 'Please do not hesitate to call upon me for anything you require, Signorina Liskard; or Madame Coron—we are at your service.'

'Thank you, but you've done so much already!' It wasn't easy to dwell on practical matters, she found, but there was the matter of her evening meal to consider, and she remembered his earlier offer as she followed the tall, lean figure with her eyes to the open doorway. 'Oh, I've just remembered; is it all right for me to go and borrow from Madame Coron's store cupboard for something to make my evening meal?'

He turned in the doorway, resting one hand on the edge of the door while he looked across at her in the cool, shady little room, and it was possible to detect a hint of speculation in his eyes for a second or two before he spoke. 'Yes, of course, *signorina*,' he said. 'But surely you will not wish to have the trouble of preparing a meal after you have travelled so far. Perhaps you will give me the pleasure of your company for dinner this evening.'

It was not at all what Troy expected when she asked about borrowing the means to make herself a meal, and yet, when she thought about it, it had always been on the cards. Nor could she truthfully claim that she would rather cook her own meal than share one prepared by Madame Coron, so, yielding to what she saw as the inevitable, she smiled a little uncertainly and nodded acceptance.

'Thank you, I'd like to very much, Signor Gaffori— just for this evening.'

He did not comment on her continued use of the formal title beyond a briefly arched brow, but inclined his head in a brief bow of acknowledgement as he turned to go. 'But of course, *mia cara signorina*,' he said. 'Just for this evening.'

CHAPTER THREE

TROY was finding it all too easy to forget about her grandfather's unfinished book, except for a few half-hearted attempts she had made at taking notes during the first couple of days. It was such a temptation to sit instead up on the hillside among the scented warmth of the maquis and gaze at the scenery. She had sat as she was now, twirling the same sprig of lavender between her fingers, for some time, unconscious of the passing of time or anything else as she revelled in the miles of rugged mountain landscape around her.

Below her, on the lowest slopes, were the thriving Gaffori vineyards, a pale green circlet between two broad sweeps of rainbow-hued shrubs, one above and one below the narrow stony road that squirmed, serpent-like, around the mountain. Higher up the mountain, where the air was more chill, loomed the forests of dark pine and fir, scarred by fire but still impressively thick and thriving for all that, and reaching almost to the summit where snow lingered all year, except for a very short time in the hottest days of summer.

Once or twice during the past two weeks Troy's conscience had reminded her with niggling insistence that she was making very little progress on her grandfather's book while she continued to simply pass the time by enjoying the scenery. But she was so captivated by the island, and by Nemio in particular, that it was very difficult to bring her mind to settling down to work.

It was so much more pleasurable to walk or simply laze amid the heady scents of the maquis and take in the magnificence of the scenery, ignoring the virgin pages of her notebook, and just dreaming. Corsica was a country that encouraged dreamers, she mused as she put the prickly-stiff lavender head to her nose and breathed in its scent; she could be forgiven for being so lazy.

Nevertheless the thought persisted that she really ought to make an effort soon, even if only to salve her conscience on the occasions when Lucien Gaffori asked what progress she had made so far. She had not actually lied to him, just been evasive, but she sometimes suspected that he knew how she spent her time.

Her grandfather would have understood her feelings exactly, for it had been he who filled her head with the wonder and matchless beauty of Corsica, and for much the same reasons, Troy thought Lucien would probably understand too. She had not seen a great deal of her host since her arrival almost two weeks before, but she was relieved that so far their infrequent meetings had been without further incident. She could not have stayed so long if her initial penchant for misunderstanding had been repeated each time he came near her.

It was while she was musing on their first traumatic meeting that something caught her eye down below on the road. A lorry was coming round the bend, slowly, as it was necessary to travel on the steep mountain roads, and distance subdued the excruciating sounds made by its labouring engine as it negotiated the bend.

It was the fact of it stopping immediately after it turned that held her attention, and she wondered at first if the engine had given up after the climb. But then she noticed a man drop nimbly from the tailboard at the back, pulling a small bag after him, then dive immediately into the dense concealing mass of undergrowth beside the road.

Apparently aware that his passenger was away, the lorry driver went on, and the man had so quickly disappeared that Troy would probably have taken no further notice of the incident if her attention had not been caught once again when the man suddenly reappeared,

much closer to where she was sitting, but still some
distance lower down.

An expanse of the prolific undergrowth had been
burnt off to ground level; a method that the shepherds
sometimes used to create new pasture for their flocks.
By burning the maquis, new shoots sprang up and provided fresh cropping for the animals, and she could already see the pale green of new growth among the
scorched brushwood.

It was on the open terrain that Troy spotted the man
again, bent almost double now and running in a curious
darting movement, so unmistakably furtive that she
could not be other than intrigued, and shading her eyes
she followed his progress curiously. Shelter was limited
on the scorched ground and his antics frankly interested
her, as it soon became clear that he was heading in the
direction of the Gaffori place, and she wondered who on
earth he could be.

A truant worker perhaps, returning from some unauthorised jaunt, or an errant husband, or—— There
Troy put a stop to further speculation before her imagination took over and she began indulging in the same
kind of fantasy that had given her such a wrong impression of Lucien Gaffori. She had been badly mistaken in
Lucien's case, and without doubt she would be equally
so in this man's case, but she was still intrigued enough to
watch and see what he did next.

Beyond the wild mass of the maquis, men and women
moved like toy figures among the vines, and Troy reflected for a moment on the possibility of the man being
seen by the field workers, despite his efforts to remain
concealed. His eventual purpose puzzled her as she
watched him seek shelter once more among the taller
growing shrubs, and she had to know about him now.

Where the terraces had been cleared to make way for
the vines, the bushes had been cut back ruthlessly and
an area of shorter growing plants was all that survived,

making a long narrow border around the entire depth of the vineyard. An approach to the house without being seen was, she would have thought, impossible, and yet the fleeting figure among the maquis, whoever he was, seemed to have that in mind.

While Troy watched curiously, he ducked and scurried along the narrow border then suddenly disappeared from her sight among the cluster of outhouses that surrounded the main house. By now she was so thoroughly involved in whatever it was the man intended, that she got up and started down the hillside, also in the direction of the house.

She could hardly demand to know what he was doing there, if she saw him, but at least she might have the chance of seeing him at closer quarters and discovering who he was and why he chose such an unconventional method of approach. It was hard to imagine that any visitor expected by Lucien Gaffori would arrive on the back of a lorry and then sneak up to the house like a fugitive from justice.

'Mademoiselle, mademoiselle!'

Shrill childish voices struck a familiar note and Troy caught sight of two small figures running along the narrow path that formed a boundary between the vines and the encroaching scrub. Waving a hand to them, she descended sharply into the mass of brushwood and lost sight of them at once, though Jérome's small piping voice could still be heard as she made her way through to the path.

'Les chèvres, mademoiselle!'

Still trying to translate what it was he was saying to her, Troy found she was suddenly in the path of a herd of fleeing goats that came leaping down the steep slope, heedless of anyone in their way. There must have been about twenty of them, nimble-footed, with black demonic masks on pale faces, long back-curved horns and pointed quivering beards.

They were harmless, of course, but seen en masse as they were, rather frightening, and she was undecided which way to step to avoid them. The children had apparently driven them down from the higher terraces, and the goats were intent only on escape; moving either way was useless anyway, because these animals came without pause and swooped around both sides of her, bleating loudly.

Troy put her hands over her ears and stood where she was, momentarily overpowered by a smell that stifled even the scents of the maquis, brushed by rough hairy coats and warily conscious of those wicked horns that came much too close for comfort. Then, when the last of them had passed, a careless step was her undoing. A thoughtless step back to watch the stragglers take off after the rest of the herd and she lost her footing on the rough uneven ground.

Unable to stop herself, she rolled downwards with her own momentum until she was brought up, breathless and momentarily stunned, against the sharp spines of a gorse bush. There was silence for a moment, complete and utter silence, and then she heard the scampering of feet and the sound of heavy breathing. The children, she thought, breathless from chasing the goats, but when she looked up after a second or two the children had gone.

Their voices came to her distantly as she tried to get her breath back, shrill and garrulous, and she shook her head as she got to her feet. Her arms were bare from the elbow down and were as dusty as her yellow shirt, but they seemed unmarked; she would probably have a few bruises later, but apart from a slight scratch on one cheek from the unfriendly gorse, she had come off lightly.

Of the goats there was no sign, only the distant complaint of their bleating downhill, and Troy sped them on their way with a few very uncomplimentary thoughts. She was brushing soil from her clothes when she looked up at the sound of voices coming closer, and saw Lucien Gaffori running down the slope towards her, almost as nimbly as those wretched goats, followed at a distance by the Vincentello children.

His anxious expression puzzled her, until it began to dawn on her suddenly that the children must have fetched him, probably from somewhere close by, since he obviously hadn't come all the way from the house. He came to a halt, facing her and frowning slightly, as if the sight of her on her feet and apparently unharmed came as a surprise to him.

'Troy?' He added the ghost of an 'a' to her name as he always did, and taking one of her hands into both his he held it while he looked into her face. 'Are you hurt?'

It was unexpected to find him so anxious, and also oddly gratifying, and she did nothing about freeing her hand, even though by now the two children had joined them and were standing just a little way off regarding them with undisguised curiosity.

'I'm O.K., thank you,' she told Lucien, and cautiously touched the scratch on her cheek with a finger-tip. 'I tripped, that's all, Lucien, I'm not hurt.'

'The children said that you were lying on the ground —that the goats——' He half turned and glanced at the two small curious faces, then shrugged. Letting go her hand, he thrust both his own into his pockets. 'I imagined you seriously hurt, it is a surprise to find you on your feet and apparently unharmed.'

'I'm sorry.' Troy brushed energetically at her soiled jeans, and shook back the untidy riot of red-brown hair from her face. 'I'm sorry you were taken away from—whatever it was you were doing when there was no need. The children were chasing the goats and I got in the way of the brutes, but they didn't harm me. I missed my footing when I turned to make sure they'd gone.'

A white shirt gave his tanned complexion a distinctly swarthy look and combined with dark slacks and a sleeveless suede jacket he suggested the mountain brigand she had first suspected him of being, so that she shook her head hastily to dismiss the illusion. It was too disturbing to think of him in any way but as her landlord for the next few weeks.

It was then that he noticed the scratch on her cheek for the first time and he reached out to turn her face to him, using the tips of his fingers. His touch tingled against her skin with unexpected effect and she felt herself shiver slightly. 'You have scratched your face,' he said, and took a large white handkerchief from a pocket while he spoke, applying it as a pad to her cheek. 'Better get it attended to as soon as you return, in case it becomes infected. Please,' he added, taking her hand and pressing it to the handkerchief to hold it in place, 'keep it covered until it has stopped bleeding.'

'But it's only a scratch——'

'Nevertheless it is better attended to,' Lucien insisted before she could protest further. 'Madame Coron will find something to put on it if you go and see her.'

'There's really no need to bother her,' Troy argued. 'I've probably got something in the car first-aid box that will do it.'

He shrugged, a glimmer of smile on his mouth. '*Benissimo*,' he said. 'It is for you to say!'

It needed only a glimpse of raised black brow to remind her that she had been rather less than gracious about his concern, and there was a faint colour in her cheeks when she looked at him again. 'I'm sorry, that wasn't very civil of me, was it?' she said with impulsive frankness. 'But I really don't need to bother Madame Coron, Lucien, and I'm very sorry you were taken away from something important only to find me all in one piece.'

For a second the black eyes regarded her steadily and she found it easier to resume brushing down her jeans than look at him. 'I am only too glad that it was a false alarm,' he said. 'Naturally I was concerned when I was told that you had been injured and that you were unconscious upon the ground.'

Once more Troy experienced an unexpected sense of satisfaction at his being so concerned, and she smiled as she held his handkerchief to her grazed cheek. 'As you see, the children got quite the wrong impression—I'm right as rain!'

'I am glad!'

It was because the black eyes had such a deeply disturbing glow in their depths that Troy turned hastily to look for her notebook and pen, dropped when she rolled down the hill. But she had no idea, as she turned to move past him, that her shirt had become snagged on the spiny branches of the gorse bush behind her, and the second she turned, the material held her back, then tore in a long ragged tear along part of the left side of her shirt and half way across her back.

'Oh no!'

She could not see the damage, only feel the warm air on her skin, and she could guess it was a pretty big tear, but the worst part was knowing Lucien would see it as just one more in a chain of embarrassing incidents. Catching the sudden bright laughter in his eyes, she actually hated him for a moment, and the sound of childish giggles when realisation dawned on Jérome and Marie, was the last straw; she turned to him.

'Oh, why did *you* have to be here when it happened?'

She did not for the moment realise the unreasonableness of the question, and she drew back sharply when Lucien reached out to try and free her from the unfriendly spines. But he held her arm firmly for a second until she stopped resisting him, then reached round and gently unhooked the shirt, trying as he did so to close the gap in the material.

'It's no good!'

The touch of his fingers troubled her almost more

than the damage to her shirt, and she glanced at him only briefly when he gave up trying. 'It seems,' he observed, not without irony, 'that you are in need of my assistance after all, eh? Come—put this on!'

He had taken off his suede jacket, she realised, and was trying to get her to put her arms into it. She did so after a moment's hesitation, and the softness of suede settled warmly about her shoulders. 'Thank you.'

'It will protect your modesty until you are safely returned to the house,' he told her, and made little attempt to hide his amusement. His hands were still on her shoulders and strong hard fingers pressed into her flesh, until she moved out of their reach, then he looked vaguely surprised at her response. 'You were angry about something,' he guessed, but did not appear unduly concerned about it. 'Do you dislike wearing my jacket, Troy?'

Too unsure of what she felt at the moment, Troy shook her head. 'Of course not,' she denied. 'I'm neither angry nor silly enough to mind wearing your jacket. I just wish I didn't keep making an idiot of myself and giving you an excuse to laugh at me, that's all, Lucien!'

'I am sorry.'

Turning her head brought his face much too close for comfort, and she quickly turned back again. 'Why should you be?' she asked with an unsteady laugh. 'I'm the one who keeps doing stupid things!'

It was unexpected when he turned her to face him and she tried not to notice the smile that still hovered about his mouth. But when he spoke it was with apparent seriousness and so quietly that it was doubtful if the two children heard what he was saying. 'I would quite gladly take time to deny that at length,' he told her, 'but I have left Louis Vincentello in the middle of a rather important discussion and I must get back to him; another time, however——' He touched her cheek lightly with a fingertip. 'Meanwhile you will not forget to see Madame Coron for something to put on your scratches, eh?'

'I'll remember,' Troy agreed hastily, and pulled the suede jacket more closely about her shoulders as she moved past him in the direction of the upward path. 'Thank you, Lucien.' She turned almost at once, remembering that he had come from the same direction himself, and spoke impulsively. 'Aren't you coming back this way?'

The black eyes held hers steadily for a second or two and she felt the more rapid beat of her heart as she tried hard not to look away. 'I shall go across this way, Troy, it will be quicker for me. I will see you later, eh?'

'Oh yes, of course.' Troy wished it need not have sounded quite so much as if she was asking him to walk back with her, and she shook her head slowly. 'I'm sorry you were brought all this way for nothing,' she said, 'but I didn't realise that the children——'

'Ah! *Non c'è di che!*' One big hand dismissed her apologies lightly. '*Ciao*, Troy!'

'*Ciao!*' She fluttered a hand in response and as she turned once more to climb the sloping path to the house she had the strangest sense of being watched. It could have been the Vincentello children, but she thought not, and she dared not turn and check. As for the man she had seen sneaking along through the undergrowth—she never even gave him another thought.

Troy winced, because although the lotion was eventually soothing to her scratched cheek, at the first application it stung sharply, and Madame Coron murmured sympathetically in her own tongue. She had not minded in the least being asked to render first aid, and had offered to put on the lotion herself without being asked. She was a friendly woman and always ready to help in any way she could.

'It's nothing very much,' Troy insisted as she smiled her thanks, 'but Monsieur Gaffori was so emphatic

about asking you for something to put on it that I
thought I'd better do as he said, just in case he checks up
on me.'

As usual, she thought the housekeeper understood
only the gist of what she said, but they got along together very well, despite occasional slight difficulties
with language. Madame Coron was always ready to
recommend the best shops, and to suggest local recipes
that she thought Troy might like to try her hand at. She
was very fond of young people, she had confided during
one conversation, but had never had a family of her own.
She was never happier than when her employer's sister
and her family visited him from Italy—the young ones
delighted her.

Troy had taken off Lucien's jacket and it was draped
over the back of a chair in the big sunny kitchen while
Madame Coron ministered to her grazed face, and the
housekeeper eyed the torn shirt with regret. 'It will be
difficult to repair, *mademoiselle*,' she told her. 'Such a
pity!'

'I was rather attached to it,' Troy confessed with a
grimace, 'but it can't be helped, I'll have to get another
one.'

'Have you also a hurt to your back, *mademoiselle*?'
she asked, and Troy attempted to look over her own
shoulder without success.

'Frankly I don't know,' she said. 'I can't see, but I
can't feel anything, so I imagine I'm unscathed. Monsieur Gaffori was very gentle when he unsnagged me, so
I'm probably not scratched.'

'*Naturellement, mademoiselle!*' Light careful fingers
explored the flesh beneath the torn fabric, and once more
Madame Coron murmured in her own tongue, following
with an explanation in her stilted English. 'There is no
mark, you are most fortunate, *mademoiselle*, that Monsieur Gaffori was so—gentle, eh?'

'Yes, I suppose I am,' Troy allowed, remembering

how amusing Lucien had found the situation too, despite how gentle he had been. 'But I do wish I needn't have made an exhibition of myself while he was within calling distance! It happens so often that I'm beginning to think I'm fated to look a fool whenever he's around!'

'*Comment, mademoiselle?*'

Troy shook her head and smiled. 'Nothing really,' she said. 'I was just complaining about my clumsiness.'

'Ah!' The housekeeper nodded her understanding, then pointed to an old-fashioned coffee pot that stood steaming beside the cooker, and raised her brows enquiringly. 'You will have *café* after your—disturbance, *mademoiselle*, eh?'

'Lovely!' The offer was not unexpected, and Troy accepted it without hesitation, but glancing down at her torn shirt, she pulled a face. 'But if you'll give me a moment, I'd like to slip across to the cottage and change into another shirt.'

'*Mais oui, naturellement, mademoiselle!* I shall be here!'

Troy felt it wasn't really necessary to put on Lucien's jacket again just to make the short trip across the yard to the cottage, so she simply slipped out by the back door, hoping the handyman, François, was not anywhere around, watching with his customary leer; but running with her arms crossed over her breast just in case he was.

The door of the cottage was never locked, it was too far from anywhere for there to be much chance of intruders, so she simply raised the latch and went in. By now the layout of the cottage was familiar to her and she did not hesitate, but went straight upstairs to the bedroom she had chosen for her own, and to save time she started to unbutton her torn shirt as she walked into the room.

She already had the top two buttons unfastened when she heard a noise overhead that made her stop dead in her tracks and look upwards. It was quite unmistakable, the floorboards in the bathroom up on the next floor had creaked as they always did when someone walked over them, and she held her breath for a moment in sheer stunned surprise before letting it out again. Then she stood staring up at the bedroom ceiling and blinking uncertainly.

Forgotten until this moment, the man she had seen arrive on the back of a lorry immediately sprang to mind again, and she caught her breath once more. She had almost convinced herself that he could not have been anything worse than a truant workman from the fields, but now that she knew there was an intruder in the cottage she was convinced she had been wrong.

Her heart was thudding and her legs shook as she tiptoed to the door and peeped out. The stairs that gave access to the upper floor where the bathroom was were right next to the bedroom door, but she could see only the first couple of treads and nothing else. She would have to take the chance of his being on his way down, and get back to the house if she could, or heaven knew what he might do. Madame Coron could summon help if it was necessary, but Troy felt horribly alone and vulnerable in her present position.

The stairs down to the ground floor creaked alarmingly as she knew from experience, but she would have to chance that, and she stepped quickly out of the bedroom doorway and across the tiny space between it and the top of the stairs, moving as swiftly and as silently as possible.

She did not even make it to the first step, however, for a man's voice murmured something almost in her ear, making her gasp aloud and step sideways instinctively, regardless of the dangerous nearness of the stairs. At once a hand clasped over her wrist and attempted to draw her back, but surprise and suspicion brought her close to panic and she struggled free, almost falling the length of the staircase as she stumbled clumsily in her flight.

'*Signorina!*'

His cry followed her as she sped swiftly across the little *salon* and straight through the half-open door into the yard beyond, forcing her shaking legs to carry her. The back way into the house had never before seemed so far away, and she fumbled with the handle before the door would open, flinging it wide when it yielded at last, and going straight in, making for the kitchen where she knew Madame Coron to be.

But she had taken only a few steps and had not even emerged from below the main staircase when a pair of strong arms put a stop to her headlong rush, making her think for a moment that her attempt at escape had been in vain. She struggled furiously against the hold of hard fingers that gripped her arms, but their grip was relentless and refused to let her go. It was the slight shake they gave her that served to bring back a modicum of self-control and she stopped struggling, though her breathing was still rapid and uneven.

'Troy!' The grip on her arms eased slightly, but she was given another light shake that banished the last remnants of her panic. 'Troy, what is the matter? What has frightened you so?'

For a moment Troy gazed up into Lucien's dark frowning face in vague disbelief, then she shook her head and glanced over her shoulder at the still open door. Instinct made her want to hug close to him in sheer relief, and the fact that the hands that held her had a more gentle touch now added to the temptation.

'There's someone—a man, in my cottage,' she told him breathlessly, and shook her head more firmly when he looked doubtful. 'It's true, Lucien, he tried to grab me as I came down the stairs, but I shook him off and ran over here!'

His brief scrutiny reminded her how dishevelled she

must look, and she instinctively put a hand to the gaping neck of her shirt, holding it together because her fingers were still too unsteady to refasten it. 'Not François?' he asked, and the look in his eyes when he put the question gave Troy a sudden sensation of chill along her spine as she shook her head hastily.

'No, it wasn't François, I'm sure, I'd have known if it was him.'

She could have coped with François, she told herself, almost certain she was right, for he was something she recognised and understood, no matter how repellent she found him. It was the element of mystery about the man in the cottage that had frightened her; the memory of his secret arrival and his furtive efforts to remain unseen. But there was still doubt in Lucien's mind, she could tell it from his eyes as he looked down at her steadily, and she shook her head impatiently.

'I saw a man when I was sitting up on the hillside, just before the Vincentello children drove the goats down,' she explained, still in the same breathless voice. 'He had a lift on a lorry and it let him off at the bend just before the vineyard starts. I watched him, sneaking along through the maquis towards the house—he obviously didn't want to be seen by the people in the fields, but he wouldn't realise I was up there. It must be the same man, Lucien, though I can't think why he chose the cottage to burgle and not the house.'

His eyes narrowed slightly, as if he finally believed her, and after a moment or two he released her arms and took both her hands instead, holding them tightly for a moment. 'Go and find Madame Coron,' he told her, 'while I discover who your visitor is and what he is doing here.'

'He might be——'

'He might be anyone, Troy,' he interrupted coolly, 'it is for me to discover, eh?'

'But be careful!'

She had spoken impulsively, suddenly fearful that the man might be armed, and she saw the way Lucien's black eyes warmed and glowed, as a ghost of a smile flitted across that wide sensual mouth. 'I shall come to no harm, Troy, though I will not pretend that I am not flattered by your concern for me. Now—will you please go and sit with Madame Coron in the kitchen while I investigate your intruder?'

Troy nodded, far from happy now that something was being done about it, although he was perfectly capable of looking after himself she had no doubt. Recalling something about the intruder suddenly, she turned and called after him as he reached the outer door.

'Oh, Lucien!' He turned and she spread her hands in a vaguely helpless gesture as she spoke. 'For what it's worth,' she said, 'I think he's Italian. I remember he called me *signorina*,' she added hastily when his frown deepened.

She could not be absolutely sure from where she stood, but Troy thought he smiled briefly as he raised a hand in acknowledgement of the information, then he turned once more and disappeared into the shadows beneath the stairway that concealed the rear door, while Troy watched him go, biting her lip anxiously. Something, and she wished she knew what it was, niggled at her mind, something concerning the fact of the man possibly being Italian; but all that really remained clear was the fact that he had grabbed her as soon as she appeared, and she had fled without even getting a look at him.

The kitchen seemed comfortingly familiar and Madame Coron was frankly curious, for she must have gathered that something was amiss when she heard them in the hall; they had been standing quite near the kitchen door. Gathering her self-control, Troy thankfully accepted the chair offered to her, and finally gave in to the trembling unsteadiness in her legs.

'Mademoiselle!' Strong coffee was poured and put before her before the housekeeper asked the inevitable question, sitting facing her across the scrubbed wooden table. *'Qu'est-ce qu'il y a, mademoiselle?'*

Troy's grimace was a little shamefaced when she considered her hasty flight from the cottage, but explanations were inevitable and at least she was sure of Madame Coron's sympathy and understanding. 'I had an intruder,' she said. 'There was a man in the cottage; upstairs in the bathroom, and he tried to grab me as I came out of the bedroom.'

'Oh, *mon dieu*!' Bright dark eyes looked at her inquisitively above the hands that covered an open mouth, despite the expression of scandalised horror. 'But who, *mademoiselle*? Who could be such a man?'

Troy took a steadying sip of thick black coffee, hot from the hob, and shook her head. 'That's what Monsieur Gaffori's gone to find out,' she said, and once more glanced anxiously across at the door. 'I only hope the man isn't armed, or too desperate.'

The same thing had obviously occurred to Madame Coron; she was very attached to her employer, and her dark eyes clouded for a moment with the depth of her concern. 'But Monsieur will call upon François with certainty,' she said, and Troy wished she could believe it.

'It has to be the same man I saw when I was up on the hillside earlier,' Troy said, talking as much for her own benefit as to enlighten the housekeeper. 'A lorry brought him as far as the bend in the road, then he was very careful not to let himself be seen while he made his way across here to the house—at least I thought he was coming to the house.' The fact that he had not still puzzled her. 'I think he's Italian,' she added, almost carelessly, and looked at Madame Coron curiously when she heard her catch her breath.

'Italien? You say this man is *Italien*?'

'Well, I'm assuming he is,' Troy said, cautious suddenly because of something in the other woman's voice. 'When he called after me he used "*signorina*" instead of "*mademoiselle*" as I'd expect a Corsican to do.'

'Because he is not Corsican, but Italian, Troy, that is why!'

The door had been ajar, but it now stood wide open and Lucien stood for a moment in the opening before he came across the kitchen to join them, and there was a certain look in Madame Coron's eyes as she got to her feet that added to Troy's discomfiture. There was something about Lucien himself too, a glittering look in his black eyes that was hard to interpret accurately, but could have been a mood between exasperation and amusement.

'He *is* Italian?' She glanced at Madame Coron, seeking some guidance, for there was something about the situation, she thought, that the other woman understood and she did not. 'Lucien——'

'Had you not discarded my jacket before you went to the cottage,' Lucien interrupted her quietly, 'my reputation might not have suffered such damage, *mia cara*!' He reached for the suede jacket that she had left draped over the back of a chair and stood for a moment with it dangling from one finger while he regarded her with gleaming black eyes.

Troy continued to stare at him uncomprehendingly. 'Lucien, what are you *talking* about?' Impatience was beginning to overcome bewilderment and her blue eyes showed him how it was, though it seemed not to trouble him too much.

He draped the jacket across her shoulders once more and shook his head. 'Your—intruder will be joining us in just a moment, Troy, and when he does you may be as violent as you wish towards him! You have my permission to attack him as furiously as your injured pride urges you to—I shall not raise a finger to defend him!'

All Troy's impatient frustration was directed at

Lucien himself at the moment, but there were certain discomfiting suspicions niggling at her mind; suspicions that were encouraged by the sounds of someone out in the hall making use of the telephone. A male voice, light and lyrical and speaking in Italian, but kept low, as if hoping to remain unheard in the kitchen.

'I mean what I say, Troy,' Lucien insisted, forestalling her questions. 'Although I can imagine the kind of impression it must have given to see you appear suddenly, running from my house with your clothes torn half from your back and your hair as dishevelled as an urchin!'

Troy struggled with her patience, despairing of the warmth of colour that showed in her cheeks as she rolled her hands tightly and faced his half-smile and gleaming black eyes. 'Lucien, who *is* he?'

'A fugitive from parental wrath,' he informed her with a typically Corsican relish for drama. 'He is my nephew, Troy—Pietro Gerolamo!'

CHAPTER FOUR

IT was quite easy, Troy found, to understand why Lucien had so readily accepted his nephew's sudden and unexpected appearance, even when he knew he had run away from his home, for some reason Troy had not yet discovered. Pietro Gerolamo was almost eighteen years old and possessed of an irresistible combination of confident maturity and boyish charm, a state of affairs of which he was not only fully aware but quite prepared to take advantage of.

He was good-looking in a typically Latin way, with dark eyes and thick glossy black hair. He was also endowed with some of the same arrogant confidence that typified his uncle, but he had none of Lucien's ruggedness and Troy suspected that very little of his Corsican grandfather had rubbed off on Pietro. But he had a youthful attraction and a bouncing optimism that was irresistible, and Troy liked him on sight.

He had apologised to her so profusely and earnestly when Lucien introduced them that she had not even thought of being angry about the fright he had given her by appearing so unexpectedly in her cottage. She had briefly forgotten even the fact that he had arrived at all when someone knocked on her door the following morning, and automatically assumed that the caller would be either Lucien or Madame Coron.

Seeing Pietro standing there when she opened the door was such a surprise that for a moment she simply looked at him rather vaguely. 'Good morning,' she said automatically.

'Good morning, Troy!' A dazzling smile illuminated the handsome brown features, and he extended one hand

63

towards her, holding a posy of wild cyclamen. 'For you!'

Hastily gathering her wits, Troy took them from him and smiled, touching the cool pink petals to her nose for a moment while she recovered herself. 'Thank you, they're lovely!' she said. 'Thank you very much, Sig——'

'If you call me anything but Pietro,' the young man warned with another smile, 'I shall believe that you have not yet forgiven me for yesterday!'

It was quite spontaneous when she stepped back to allow him through the doorway, and he followed her unhesitatingly into the little *salon* with the air of one who is thoroughly familiar with his surroundings. Holding the flowers in both hands, Troy once more made a pretence of smelling them, then she looked up at him curiously, taking the posy of flowers as a subject of conversation because she felt curiously ill at ease with him.

'These are wild ones, aren't they?' she asked. 'You must have been out and about very early this morning.'

'Quite early,' he admitted, and his dark eyes watched her as she looked around for something in which to put his offering; the delicate blooms would not last very long out of water. 'Not before Lucien was, though,' he said. 'But he doesn't bring you flowers, does he, Troy?'

He asked the question with such an air of innocence that Troy was bound to believe that its intent had been quite the reverse, and she hastily avoided his eyes. He spoke better English than Lucien did, but without that rather attractively fluid accent. His pronunciation was a more clipped and polished one, much more English in intonation, as if he had spoken the language for longer and was less a stranger to it.

Troy avoided answering his query about Lucien not bringing her flowers by picking up a small delicate porcelain vase and setting her posy in it, primping up the tiny pink blooms into some kind of arrangement before standing back to admire them. 'There,' she said, head to one side, 'they look just perfect in that, don't they?'

'Very pretty,' Pietro agreed absently. He was watching her still, with a faintly quizzical expression that Troy was aware of but chose to ignore for the moment, and he was balanced with familiar ease on the edge of a small marble-topped table. Not once did he take his eyes off her while she carried the vase of cyclamen over to the window and set them down on the narrow sill. 'Is it really true that you are here in Nemio to write a book, Troy?' he asked.

Obviously Lucien had told him that much, but she could not help wondering if he regretted letting her have the cottage, since it had meant him having to explain her presence to his nephew. Quite clearly Pietro was more than a little intrigued with the idea of his uncle letting rooms to passing strangers, and he would not be backward in trying to discover the reason, unless she was very much mistaken.

Troy gave the flowers another gentle primp while she answered him, and did not turn round from the window. 'It's partly true,' she said, and heard him chuckle to himself.

'Ah!'

'I'm here to *complete* a book,' she told him quickly. 'My grandfather started a work on Corsican wild life more than two years ago, but he hadn't finished it when he died last year. I'm hoping to do that for him, if I'm able to.'

'Ah, I see, so you *are* writing a book!'

'Yes, you could say I am.' Troy had no need to guess what alternative ideas he had for her being there as his uncle's guest, and she was not at all happy about it. 'As a matter of fact,' she went on, unable to resist letting him know, 'it was because I was out on the mountainside that I saw you arrive yesterday. I saw you drop down from the back of a lorry and come creeping through the maquis towards the house. The way you behaved I thought you were an escaped convict or something just as unsavoury.'

'Which is why you were so startled when I spoke to you,' Pietro said, and used his fine eyes to good effect while he apologised once more. 'I am sorry, Troy, truly I am.'

'Oh——' She shrugged uneasily, remembering how she had gone running across to the house for help, and how wildly she had struggled with Lucien before she realised who he was. 'I panicked and ran,' she told him, laughing to relieve the uneasiness she felt. 'I can't think why I reacted as I did, I'm not usually such a nervous individual, but I suppose it was seeing you earlier, and thinking you were up to no good out there. I was rather edgy.'

Pietro pulled a face, but he was not nearly as discomfited as Troy expected at learning he had been spotted making that surely unnecessarily melodramatic arrival at his uncle's house. 'You could blame that on a Corsican taste for the dramatic,' he told her without a trace of embarrassment. 'My grandfather is Corsican, you know.'

'Yes, I know, Lucien told me.'

Troy spoke absently and without thinking, but there was something about the sudden elevation of Pietro's black brows that made her wish she had been less impulsive. He sat with one foot hooked carelessly over the gilded stretcher between the table legs and appeared completely at ease, and quite frankly curious.

'Have you known Lucien for very long?' he asked, then laughed and shook his head when she looked wary. 'You seem to know quite a lot about one another for strangers,' he explained. 'Lucien mentioned to me that you had a French grandfather, and now you tell me that you already knew that Nonno Gaffori is Corsican.' His slim boyish hands spread meaningly and he shrugged. 'I thought perhaps you knew each other—well.'

Once more there was little chance of mistaking the meaning behind his seemingly innocent words, and Troy hastened to put him right. 'I met Lucien for the first time two weeks ago,' she told him, and wished that bright curious gaze did not make her feel so gauchely uneasy. 'I was very nearly involved in what could have been a very serious accident, with some children who were driving the goats from the terraces. Lucien was with them, but I didn't know it until I opened my eyes afterwards and he was standing there.'

Something about the way she said it must have given Pietro a clue, for that irrepressible smile was in evidence again. 'So, *he* frightened you too, on first acquaintance,' he guessed, and Troy nodded.

'I didn't even know he spoke any English,' she remembered, 'and he looked so—fierce, standing there with that long staff in one hand, I quite expected to be attacked.' She realised how interested Pietro was in her reminiscence, and hurried on. 'In the event he told me that the friends of my grandfather that I was looking for were dead, and the younger members of the family had emigrated, so I was going to have to find somewhere else to stay.'

'So Lucien decided to become a landlord!' He chuckled as if the situation amused him and, folding his arms across his chest, he continued to watch her closely. 'Well, well! I can't help wondering, Troy, if my uncle would have proved quite so hospitable had you been twenty years older and not so pretty!'

'You're barking up quite the wrong tree, Signor Gerolamo!' Troy made the denial a little breathlessly, a fact that did not escape her visitor, and turned away, ostensibly to tidy the things on another small table behind her. 'That means——'

'Oh, I know the expression perfectly well,' Pietro informed her with a smile, and her own curiosity made her turn her head again briefly.

'You speak very good English,' she told him, impulsively frank. 'I mean more—precise than Lucien's.'

'And so I should,' Pietro explained with no trace of false modesty. 'My father is a member of the Diplomatic Corps, and he was with the Italian Embassy in London for more than six years. Gianni, my brother, and I went to an English school during that time and I still write to a friend in England.'

Troy was interested, and her smile showed him she was as she turned around to give him her full attention once more. 'You know England?'

He pulled a wry face, but his dark eyes were bright with mischief. 'I know the immediate countryside around Saint Biddulph's Priory in Surrey,' he told her, 'and a little of London, but for school holidays we were packed off to stay with Grandmother Gerolamo in Rome, so that we cannot claim to know England nearly as well as we know its language. I think Papa feared we might become too English and forget that we were the latest in the long line of Gerolamos if we were not reminded of it for a few weeks each year!'

'Oh, I see.' Troy smiled at him and saw the same response in his eyes that she had so often noticed in Lucien's when she smiled, so that she hastily avoided them. 'Well, that explains that different—intonation, of course; your accent is so very much more English than Lucien's.'

Pietro lowered one eyelid briefly and laughed, softly but with a wealth of meaning. 'Ah, but Lucien did not learn his English in the schoolroom, eh?'

'I'm sure I don't know!' Troy resumed her pretence of tidying, still watched by Pietro's interested eyes, but she found him far too much of a distraction to keep up the pretence for very long. 'Are you here for very long?' she asked after a while. 'Lucien told me that you and your brother usually sleep in the cottage when you're here, but you weren't expected this time, were you? Or Lucien wouldn't have let me have it.'

Picking up a tiny onyx figure from the table beside him, Pietro turned it over and over in his hand while he answered her, although she was aware that he glanced at her from time to time through his thick black lashes, as if he sought her response to what he was saying. 'I think there will almost certainly be some trouble about my being here,' he confessed, though not with any degree of anxiety, it seemed to Troy. 'I came without telling anyone I was coming, you see, and it is likely that someone will be coming to—persuade me to go back.'

'You ran away?' Troy put it in a nutshell, and he nodded, then gave her a glimpse of a wry but almost irresistible smile.

'I am hoping that if someone does come it will be my mother,' he confided, quite frank about his reasons. 'Papa will order me home, but Mamma will try to persuade me. I have no intention of submitting to either, you understand, but I will be much less likely to lose my temper if I am persuaded, and I am so very much more likely to say something I regret if I lose my temper.'

His frankness took Troy's breath away for a second or two. His sublime confidence was almost comical, but she guessed that his main reason for telling her so much was because he wanted someone to talk to about it, other than Lucien. His uncle had probably been less than sympathetic in the circumstances and Pietro would not like that.

'Your family will be worried about you, won't they?' she suggested, and Pietro shrugged with assumed indifference.

'Not any more,' he told her. 'Lucien made me telephone them as soon as he found me here; before even I was able to apologise to you.'

Troy recalled the sound of someone using the telephone out in the hall while Lucien was breaking the news to her that her intruder was no one more dangerous than his nephew. 'Just the same, it must have been a shock to them to realise you'd gone,' she said, and once more a light shrug proclaimed his apparent carelessness.

'I suppose so,' he allowed. 'But I had expected Lucien to be more in sympathy; he has always been so understanding about letting us sleep in the cottage and——' He shrugged his disappointment and his lower lip pursed resentfully. 'I am very disappointed in Lucien, and I have told him so—he is behaving like a parent!'

Pietro was only about four years younger than herself, and Troy could feel for him because his idol had proved to have feet of clay, but at the same time she had to see Lucien's point of view. Not that she was prepared to declare herself one way or the other at the moment, and she hoped she would never have to. It was not her concern and never would be if she could help it.

'At least you chose a wonderful place to come to,' she said, hopeful of changing the subject. 'Do you like Corsica?'

A glimmer of slightly scornful amusement in Pietro's dark eyes showed her that her ruse had been detected, but he answered her willingly enough. 'I wanted somewhere to run to,' he told her, 'and I thought Lucien would understand my point of view, that's why I chose Corsica!'

'I think maybe he does understand,' Troy told him, yielding to the inevitability of a discussion. 'But maybe he feels for your mother too, Pietro; for your family.'

'You think he's right not to stand by me?' he asked, and Troy wondered what on earth kind of answer she was supposed to give to someone she had known for less than twenty-four hours.

'I know nothing about the circumstances,' she reminded him, and went on hastily when he showed signs of remedying the situation, 'and I don't think I want to. I don't think I ought to discuss such purely family business, Pietro. After all, I'm a complete stranger, you only just met me, and this is strictly a family affair. I don't want to be involved.'

'How very British!' he jeered, then caught her hand when she started to turn away from the jibe. 'I am sorry, Troy! I should not be so selfish, I know. That is what Lucien says I am,' he added with one of his incredibly appealing smiles, 'and I suppose it's true in one way. Only I had rather depended on him to stand by me.'

Whether or not she wanted to be involved, it seemed she was going to be, and Troy just hoped that Lucien was going to understand her position if he got to hear about it, though somehow she did not think he would. She freed her hand easily enough from Pietro's and walked over to the window to look out over the vine-smothered terraces and beyond them to the endless vista of rainbow maquis and dark forest on a background of mountain peaks, their summits still tipped with snow that the spring sunshine could not melt.

Family quarrels were not what she had come to Corsica for, and briefly she resented the fact that she was being drawn inextricably into Pietro's problem with his parents and his uncle, without even knowing what it was all about. 'What have you done that made you run away from home, Pietro?' she asked, and realised that by asking she had taken the first step to complete involvement.

Pietro made no move to come and join her where she stood by the window, and she was thankful for that at least. Apparently he was still sitting on the little marble-topped table and looking cool and casual, and much less disturbed than she now suspected he was. She had no brothers and she was not accustomed to receiving the confidences of young men, and especially young men whom she had known for such a short time. But in Pietro's case there seemed to be little option for her.

'It is expected—it *was* expected that I would go on to university this year,' Pietro told her, speaking slowly and sounding as if he chose his words carefully. 'I do not want to go to university,' he went on in a flat and determined voice that somehow confirmed Troy's suspicion that he sought another and more sympathetic ear than Lucien's disappointingly intolerant one. 'I do not wish to join the Diplomatic Corps as my father did, and *his* father! I wish to grow grapes for making wine, as Lucien does and as Nonno Gaffori does. Can you understand that, Troy?

It was a difficult question to answer right off, for Troy sympathised completely with his ambition, but at the same time she could not bring herself to tell him so when she was quite sure he would use her support to bolster his argument with his family. It was Lucien's reaction that she was particularly wary of, she frankly admitted as much to herself, but it made it harder to be quite honest with Pietro, and she sought for an answer that would both satisfy him and at the same time not commit her to lending her full support.

'I can imagine just how you feel,' she told him cautiously, 'but there must be some good reason why they don't agree with your idea, Pietro. After all, it can't be because they see anything wrong with being winegrowers, because both your grandfather Gaffori and Lucien are that, so they must have some other, very strong reason for not letting you choose for yourself. Do they know how you feel—how *deeply* you feel about it?'

'It would make no difference to Papa,' Pietro told her, and Troy felt there was already a hint of resignation in his voice. 'For generations there has been a Gerolamo in the Diplomatic Corps and the tradition must not be broken! It is almost a family business,' he added with rueful irony, 'so why do I wish to break the tradition?'

'What about your brother—Gianni? Is he going into diplomacy too?'

Pietro shrugged, careless of his brother's future for the moment, because he was much too involved in his own. 'I think perhaps I have a lot of Nonno Gaffori in me after all, eh?' he asked with a ghost of a smile. 'I wish to do as *I* want, not to follow a path that others have chosen for me! If Nonno Gaffori had done so he would still be a shepherd here in the Corsican mountains!'

Troy could also see a good deal of his uncle in him as he stubbornly proclaimed his intention of going his own way, for she could quite easily imagine Lucien taking a similar stand in the same circumstances. It made it all the more difficult to understand why he had not given Pietro the support he expected from him, and there was nothing she could do to disguise the sympathy in her voice as she turned and looked up at him.

'It does seem a shame that you can't choose your own career, Pietro, I agree,' she told him. 'In the circumstances I——'

'In the circumstances you would be well advised to refrain from offering encouragement, Troy!'

Pietro said something under his breath, and both he and Troy turned swiftly at the sound of Lucien's voice from the open doorway. To Troy, who felt the hot colour flooding into her face, the situation had a certain inevitability. She realised the impression her words must have conveyed to someone hearing them out of context, as Lucien had, but before she could say anything to remedy matters, he went on speaking, addressing himself to Pietro without moving away from the doorway.

'I came over to let you know, Pietro, that your mother is coming here, to try and talk some sense into your head!'

'It will do no good,' Pietro assured him sharply. 'And you are mistaken if you think that Troy was encouraging me!'

'Allow me to know what I heard,' Lucien told him with equal shortness. 'I am capable of hearing from this distance!'

He was gone and the door closed firmly behind him before Troy could say a word in her own defence, but

Pietro was saying something in Italian. Something short and so virulent that she felt it was as well she did not understand it, then he turned and looked at her once more, his dark eyes showing concern.

'I am sorry, Troy,' he said. 'I seem to have made things difficult for you with Lucien. But rest assured that I shall explain to him at the first opportunity just how impartial you were—I promise.'

Smarting from the injustice, Troy shook her head firmly and her mouth, usually so soft and smiling, was set in a firm straight line, her blue eyes bright with as much hurt as anger as she looked at the closed door. 'Oh, please don't bother, Pietro,' she told him with a light and not quite steady laugh. 'I suppose Lucien has to be allowed to get hold of the wrong end of the stick occasionally too—I've done it often enough where he's concerned!' She caught Pietro's puzzled look and shook her head. 'It's nothing,' she told him. 'Just a kind of private joke!'

It was almost a relief to have something to concentrate on, and Troy took a more intense interest in her note-taking than she had done so far; anything was better than dwelling on Lucien's angry departure from the cottage earlier. No matter if some of the species she noted had already been recorded by her grandfather, it was simple enough to delete the duplicates, and she gave her mind determinedly to what she was doing.

Distraction was all too easily come by, however, and after a while she raised her head to follow the progress of a buzzard as it soared off into the spring-blue sky. One hand shading her eyes, she watched it climb, then hover, and she forgot about her notes in the primitive thrill of seeing the hunter spot his prey and prepare for the kill.

The bird swooped unerringly and with the grace and swiftness of an arrow, winging aloft again almost at once with some small unfortunate creature clutched in its talons. Finding the kill less thrilling than the hunt, she shivered and looked away, her notebook once more forgotten but seeking another distraction, less disturbing.

Across on another slope a goatherd shifted his flock slowly along the edge of a patch of scorched scrub, seeking better pasture, and the plaintive bleating of the animals sounded strangely like the cries of a human child. It was hard to believe that the same creatures were capable of the discordant racket that had surrounded her the day before when the Vincentello children drove them from the vineyards.

Sitting close to the taller scrub she had some shade without quite losing the advantage of the sun, and she looked around swiftly when a dog barked somewhere, breaking into the soft, everyday sounds with its strident warning. With a hand to her eyes she tried to locate it in the denseness of the maquis, but it was difficult to see very far beyond the barrier of growth predominated by spiny gorse and scented white myrtle.

Then the dog barked once more, a short, sharp snap of sound, followed by the echo of a howl that sent shivers coursing along Troy's spine and she frowned. Dogs held no terrors for her, for she had owned one ever since she was a small child, but something about this one both puzzled and disturbed her. If it was simply a village dog it could hardly be lost, for even among the profusion of scents around her, a dog could find its way home.

Then it barked again and the moan of sound that followed once more streaked an icy finger through her blood, so that she got to her feet and looked around. It was compassion as well as curiosity that took her on into the taller growing bushes that came almost as high as the top of her head, and she brushed aside the densely growing myrtle with a gesture that set it quivering and swaying in her wake.

A sound just off to her right made her turn quickly, but she saw nothing beyond the slight swaying of the bushes, where something had passed through them.

There were no more barks and only the distant bleating of goats disturbed the stillness when she stood for a moment and listened, so that she shrugged as she turned to make her way back to her place on the hillside. Obviously the dog had run off.

The sound that shattered the quiet so suddenly and alarmingly was unmistakable, even to Troy's inexperienced ear. A gunshot cracked sharply, then bounced back from the mountain in a series of diminishing echoes, and something close by set the bushes rustling without the aid of the light wind. Troy caught her breath, unwilling to believe it, for there was no hunting season in progress at the moment, and there should have been no danger from hunters.

Her heart fluttered rapidly and it was a moment before she turned and started back towards the more open ground she had left. If there was someone out there with a gun, it was safer to make sure she could be clearly seen. But she had barely taken two steps before another shot rang out and this time she distinctly heard the whistle of the bullet over her head.

Rooted to the spot with shock, Troy dared not move a muscle in case the marksman, whoever he was, mistook her for his target, and by now she was fairly sure that it was the dog she had heard. A dog running wild in the hills could all too easily become a menace to the flocks, and obviously some irate shepherd or goatherd was trying to put a stop to the animal's activities.

She still had a short distance to go before she reached the safety of open ground, but it was those few steps that she hesitated to take for fear of hearing another shot come whistling over her head or, worse, finding its target. Even turning her head might be enough to attract him and she was still trying to summon the courage to duck down and crawl on all fours when she heard someone else coming.

There was little more than a faint swishing sound to guide her, but she recognised it as the sound of a human body pushing its way through the scrub. Such was the temptation to turn and see who was coming that she momentarily forgot the marksman and she had time only to catch a glimpse of the myrtle in front of her parting to make way for someone to come through before another sharp crack echoed around the mountain.

The whistling flight of the bullet coincided with the sudden collapse of her legs and for a moment Troy had the awful thought that she had been hit, as she fell to the ground. It was only when another body fell crushingly on top of her that she realised what had happened and she lay still for a second too stunned to move, but with her heart thudding like a wild thing in her breast.

It seemed like an eternity before she dared to raise her face just a fraction and gaze at the strong brown masculine throat that was all her line of vision took in. But she was held in arms that wrapped themselves tightly around her so that she could not move, and a long lean body shielded her from anything that might come near, whether animal or bullet.

Sooner or later she was bound to move, and after a few seconds she stirred slightly and the weight that held her pressed close to the ground eased sufficiently for her to see the face of the man above her. Not that she needed to see him to recognise Lucien, but she looked up at him for a moment with her blue eyes wide, in a kind of startled naïveté, almost as if she had never seen him before.

'It will soon be safe to move,' he told her in a stunningly matter-of-fact voice. 'Vincentello has gone to tell the fool that it is a woman he is firing at and not the renegade dog he seeks to destroy.'

'He——' Troy realised how she was shaking, even with the supporting strength of his arms around her, and she flicked the tip of her tongue across her lips before she could go on. 'He almost had me just now, just before you arrived.'

'*Si, si, lo so!*' He used his own tongue possibly because he was as edgily nervous as she was herself, Troy thought, for all his matter-of-fact tone. Moving slightly, he made it easier for her to breathe, but he still had his arms about her and his lean hardness still pressed close to her side as he peered through the undergrowth in an attempt to see beyond it to the hidden marksman. 'I attempted to signal the fool, but he either misunderstood me or he is far too blind to be handling a rifle. Either way I felt sure he would have made you his target before I could get to you.' He looked down into her face, so very close to his, and his black eyes scanned her features closely. 'You are not hurt, are you, Troy?'

'I'm quite all right, Lucien, just scared silly!' She made the admission with a laugh that shivered with hysteria, and his arms tightened around her briefly, then relaxed enough for her to shift a little further away and be able to see him more clearly. 'I heard a dog barking,' she told him in a voice that was breathless with the chaos of emotion his nearness aroused in her. 'I hope he doesn't get killed.'

Lucien parted the undergrowth with one hand in a vain attempt to penetrate the density of its growth and see as far as the opposite hillside, and when he did so he leaned across her, making her once more aware of the hard, strong leanness of him. She did her best to remember that he was there simply because he had realised her danger, but the temptation to reach up and touch the small pulsing spot at the base of his brown throat was almost irresistible.

'You should hope rather that the creature is killed, Troy,' he said, still in that incredibly matter-of-fact voice, 'for sooner or later it will be either wounded or die of starvation if it is not, and you have too much compassion, I think, to wish that to happen.'

'Can't he be caught?'

Common sense would have told her that the result for the animal would be exactly the same if it was caught, but the situation she found herself in at present was not a normal one and she could not think logically. Lying huddled on the warm earth with Lucien's arms around her was not conducive to clear thinking, and she saw nothing untoward in discussing the ultimate fate of a renegade dog.

She felt curiously relaxed, despite her professed concern over the dog, and there was a strangely satisfying sense of rightness about being where she was; and when Lucien looked down at her with his deep, black eyes she saw a reflection of the same reaction there. Recognising it brought a small half-smile to her mouth and a hint of colour to her cheeks. A long finger reached up and lightly brushed aside a tendril of hair from her neck and she instinctively half-closed her eyes on the effect of it.

'You do not catch mad dogs, *piccola*,' he said softly, 'you destroy them before they do too much damage. You think too—English, eh?'

'Probably because I *am* English!' Troy retorted with breathless haste, and feeling far less indignant than her upthrust chin suggested. 'I happen to like dogs, and I don't like to think of the poor creature being shot at simply because——'

Another shot rang out, echoing round the mountain peaks and cutting short Troy's protest, and this time she would have sworn it was much further away; there was certainly no whistling bullet following on it in this instance. She looked up at Lucien questioningly after a second or two and he shook his head.

He withdrew the arm that had been beneath her, then folded both arms under him and raised his head to listen, his dark head tilted slightly to one side. 'He has changed direction,' he said, when another shot followed closely on the first. 'Perhaps the creature has been seen a little further away and is being driven off.' He sat up, resting his weight on one hand. 'I think it will be safe for us to move from here now, Troy.'

'Are you sure?' Sitting with her legs curled up under her she glanced over her shoulder at the barrier of all-concealing scrub that hid them from the marksman's view and also hid him from them, then she put a tentative hand to the front of his shirt to draw his attention to her. 'I haven't thanked you for coming to find me—to warn me,' she said in a small soft voice that was slightly unsteady. 'I'm grateful, Lucien, really, I was really scared.'

'But of course you were,' he agreed. 'Anyone would be, having a rifle fired at them; it is a frightening situation.'

Once more she glanced over her shoulder. 'Do you really think it's safe to move? He might fire across in this direction again if he sees any kind of movement.'

For a moment Lucien said nothing, but his black eyes held hers with an intensity that made her hastily look away. Easing himself over on to one elbow, he looked up into her face. 'I am quite willing to stay here for as long as you wish, Troy,' he said in his deep, lyrical English, and a hasty glance showed her that he was smiling in the way she remembered from their very first meeting. 'Are you quite comfortable as you are, or do you feel safer with my arms around you?'

It could have looked as if that was what she had in mind when she hesitated about going, Troy realised, and regretted her impulsiveness as she so often did. Then she shook her head firmly when he reached out with the obvious intention of taking her in his arms again, and scrambled quickly to her feet.

'You always must misunderstand me, mustn't you, Lucien?' she accused crossly, and took an involuntary step backwards when he got nimbly to his feet and stood for a moment brushing the clinging fragments of dried twig from his clothes.

When he looked up it was with the directness she was growing accustomed to but found none the less disconcerting for all that. His black eyes held hers unwaveringly, until it was she who broke the contact, and his voice was once more matter-of-fact with only a trace of that other deep and dangerously attractive softness.

'I am sorry if I misunderstood you, Troy——'

'You *did* misunderstand!' Troy interrupted swiftly. 'Just as you did when you heard me say about Pietro choosing his own career; you didn't stop to find out whether or not I *was* encouraging him!'

She found it so much easier to keep a rein on her emotions if she remembered reasons for criticising him, although it was not easy even then. He took a second to consider how he should answer that, and while he did so Troy was tempted to walk away, but her legs felt oddly weak and unsteady and he *had* taken the trouble and risk of coming to find her.

'It was not necessary for you to be made the recipient of Pietro's—confessions,' he told her. 'It is purely a family matter and concerns no one else.'

'Which is precisely what I was in the process of telling Pietro when you accused me of encouraging him!' Troy insisted.

Once more Lucien seemed to take time to consider, then he shook his head and smiled, a faintly ironical smile that gave his mouth a curiously vulnerable look almost as effective as Pietro's. Holding her gaze, he extended a hand towards her and Troy took it without a moment's hesitation, feeling a thrill of pleasure course through her veins when his strong fingers closed over hers.

'I am sorry,' he said simply, and Troy shook her head but said nothing, only clung to his hand while they went down through the dense growth of gorse, myrtle and honeysuckle to the lower slopes where it was all lavender, wild mint and cyclamen, and their feet crushed the growing plants and raised the incomparable scent of the maquis around them.

CHAPTER FIVE

TROY could not imagine why it took her so by surprise when Lucien issued an invitation a couple of days later to drive with him to a town called Benecollocare, but she was totally unprepared for it and the fact was quite clear from her expression—a fact that he noted with a flick of his dark brows as he waited for her answer. Benecollocare, as far as she knew, was about twenty kilometres south of Nemio through some of the wildest mountain country, and she could think of no reason why he should ask her unless he simply wished to take her for a drive.

She was with Pietro when the invitation was issued. Lucien had come and found them chatting together in the yard that divided the house from the cottage, and Pietro's reaction was quite different from hers. He obviously assumed that he was to be included and he welcomed the idea enthusiastically, urging her to accept without giving her time to gather her wits.

'Oh, but of course we will go, Troy, eh?' he said. 'It is not a very big town, but it is pleasant enough, and quite near to the coast as well as having shops and quite a few ancient buildings. We could spend a very pleasant hour or two there!'

'Just a moment!' Troy's response was deferred by Lucien's firm voice and his dark eyes were gleaming when he looked at his nephew in that compellingly arrogant way that Troy was so familiar with. 'You will not be coming, I am afraid, Pietro.'

Pietro's disappointment was evident and loudly vocal and he stared at his uncle's adamantly set mouth in disbelief as he made his protest. 'But you know I don't have my own car here, Lucien, I have no means of taking

82

Troy anywhere unless it is in your car which you do not allow me to drive! Am I to be confined to Nemio for ever because I have no means of transport?'

Ignoring the drama of the plea, Lucien obviously had no intention of changing his mind, and he shook his head firmly. 'In this instance I am afraid you are going to be disappointed,' he confirmed relentlessly. 'A telephone call is expected from Rome, from your *mamma*, and I would like you to take it for me, Pietro.'

'So that you can drive with Troy to Benecollocare!'

'I had hoped you would be obliging enough to do this for me,' Lucien informed him coolly, and Pietro looked at him suspiciously.

It was a day or two since anything had been said about his unauthorised visit to Corsica, and with youthful optimism he had probably hoped the matter was simply being allowed to drift. But studying his uncle's expression he must have known how unlikely that was. 'Surely,' he suggested, 'Mamma will wish to speak with you, Lucien; I am in disgrace, remember!'

'I agree that you are temporarily out of favour with your parents, and with good reason,' Lucien told him, not without a hint of humour, Troy was surprised to realise. 'But if you speak with your *mamma* on the telephone in my place, so that she is aware that you are taking the responsibility of—how is it?—standing in for me, then it may perhaps do something to restore you to *her* good grace at least!'

'It is Papa that I have to convince,' Pietro told him, under no delusions, but Lucien's deep cool voice for all its hint of humour was none the less implacable.

'Win over your *mamma*, and you have almost won the battle,' he advised Pietro with confidence, and apparently Pietro could find no valid argument.

The irritable shrug of his shoulders, however, left his feelings in little doubt and he could not resist a last comment. 'I do not——' he began.

'There will be no argument,' Lucien declared firmly. 'For the moment I am *in loco parentis* and I would much prefer that you speak with your *mamma* when she telephones. It is possible that even at a distance she may——'

He shrugged his broad shoulders as if the burden of even temporary parenthood weighed too heavily, and the gleam in his black eyes must have carried warning enough, for Pietro subsided. Complaining to himself in Italian and looking very much a sulky schoolboy, he gave in with a resigned lift of his shoulders, while the quelling frown that had silenced him was dispelled when Lucien turned back to Troy.

'*Would* you like to drive to Benecollocare with me, Troy?' he asked, and spared his nephew another brief glance. 'Or would you prefer the company of a chaperone?'

He must have realised that the role of chaperone was the one Pietro had allotted to him, and Troy could not help wondering if realising it had influenced his manner. In the event she did not hesitate to deny her nervousness at the idea of driving with him, and she shook her head firmly. 'You know perfectly well I don't need a chaperone, Lucien!' she told him, and noted the gleam of satisfaction that showed in his eyes for a moment.

'That is what I hoped you would say,' he admitted, and completely ignored Pietro's soulful gaze while he consulted his wrist-watch. 'I am prepared to start as soon as you are ready,' he told her, and it was instinctive when Troy glanced down at the green-flowered cotton dress she was wearing.

'I'd better go and change this dress first,' she said, and noticed for the first time that he was more formally dressed than she had ever seen him before.

A lightweight suit in beige with shirt looked neat and very formal, except that he wore no tie and the smartly tailored jacket was unfastened. He no longer looked like a farm-worker or a brigand, but every inch the successful businessman he was, and it gave her a curious sense of distance, as if she saw a different man altogether—until he eyed the green cotton dress with evident approval.

'Is that necessary?' he asked. 'That dress is perfect!'

Troy brushed down the skirt with slightly unsteady hands and laughed, tossing her thick hair back in a gesture of unconscious bravado. 'In that case,' she told him, 'I'll be no more than a few minutes!'

A finger touched his brow in a lighthearted salute. 'Then I will see you in ten minutes, eh?'

It was incredible to realise that she had almost forgotten Pietro was there, watching in obvious annoyance, but saying nothing, and she turned quickly to show at least a little sympathy before she went. 'Some other time, Pietro, eh?' she suggested, and he nodded.

'Do not feel too sorry for him,' Lucien warned her with a ghost of a smile. 'In the circumstances he cannot complain, and it is a favour to me, taking this call from my sister, eh, Pietro?' His nephew nodded agreement, although with no great enthusiasm, and Lucien put a consoling hand on his shoulder. 'And I am very grateful, *galante mio!*'

Troy said nothing, but she spared Pietro another brief smile before she went across the yard to her cottage. It would be untrue to claim that she felt Pietro's disappointment was hers too, however sorry she felt for him. She was still slightly dazed by the unexpectedness of Lucien's invitation, but she looked forward to driving with him whatever his reason for asking her.

In fact she did not discover another reason, apart from a desire for her company, until they had been driving for some time. The road they took was through cool dense pine forests and there might have been no one else on earth but the two of them, for they saw no one. Driving along narrow roads that looked as if they went on for ever between ranks of tall trees whose tops were so close together that the sky appeared as no more than a blue ribbon weaving its way above them. There was a fresh spicy smell from the trees and the earth had the rich aroma peculiar to pine forests.

The sense of isolation persisted until gradually the trees began to thin, and presently another turn of the wheel brought them out of the forest shadows and on to a downward route between slopes that were covered with the more familiar rainbow hues of the maquis. Not the taller growing shrubs and trees that predominated around Nemio, but shorter herbaceous plants that enlarged the vista and scented the air with wild mint and thyme and a dozen other perfumes she could not hope to remember.

Snatching herself back to a level of reality, Troy realised that she was being asked a question. 'Have you ever heard your grandfather speak of a man called Maurice Corsi, Troy?'

Troy took a moment. Somewhere, she thought, she had heard the name mentioned, but she could not be sure, and she looked at him curiously, wondering what he was leading up to. 'I'm not sure,' she told him. 'It seems to ring a bell somewhere, but I can't be certain.' She was intrigued because she knew he would not have asked such a question without good reason and she frowned at him enquiringly. 'Why do you ask?'

'Because we are on our way to see him!'

'Oh! Oh, I see.'

Paying calls had not been on her list of possibilities, and Troy wished she had taken the time to change her dress after all. Someone that Lucien knew was quite likely to be another businessman, and to have womenfolk who wore something more chic than printed cotton in a rather little-girl style. Lucien had seen nothing wrong with the way she looked, but that did not altogether reassure her.

Obviously her silence aroused some doubt, for he glanced at her curiously as they wound their way downward on the rocky mountain road. 'Are you not interested in meeting someone who might have known your *grandpère*?' he asked, and Troy hastened to assure him.

'Oh yes, of course I am, Lucien, it's just that—well, I wasn't expecting to visit anyone, that's all. I'm not sure that I shouldn't have changed this dress after all and smartened myself up a bit before I go visiting.'

Black eyes turned swiftly and surveyed her uncertain face, then he reached over and briefly clasped her hand with his strong warm fingers. 'Have I not said that you look very well as you are?' he asked. 'Believe me, *cara mia*!'

When he returned both hands to the wheel, Troy instinctively replaced the pressure of his fingers by clasping her hands closely together on her lap while she nodded. It was safer, she felt, to change the subject. 'Do you think this man that you know might remember Grandpère?' she asked.

'I hope so. You should like that, would you not?'

'I always like talking about him,' she said, almost naïvely frank, and Lucien smiled.

'Maurice Corsi was a good friend of my father's when they were both very much younger,' he said, 'and since both are contemporaries of your grandfather and both have been in Nemio at some time when he was there, I thought perhaps——' An eloquent shrug completed his explanation, and Troy was touched by his thoughtfulness more deeply than she would have believed possible.

Looking round at him, she smiled. 'It's very thoughtful of you, Lucien, and I shall love meeting your friend, especially if he *does*—did know Grandpère! Thank you.'

The knowledge that he had gone to the trouble of organising the trip on the offchance that she could meet a friend of her grandfather's pleased her enormously

and she made no effort to disguise the fact, a response
that obviously gave him pleasure too. Glancing briefly
over one shoulder, he drew her gaze with those irresistible black eyes and smiled, only faintly mocking.

'Also I thought that you would enjoy a change of
scenery and a drive in the mountains,' he told her, and
half-lowered one eyelid. 'And the company of your land-
lord, of course!'

That melodious mispronunciation sent a little tingle of
pleasure through her senses, and she smiled. 'Well, I
have,' she assured him. 'I've enjoyed it enormously—
both the drive and the company!' It was incredible how
disturbing she found him at such close quarters, and in
the circumstances she did her best to quell the rising
excitement that filled her by raising more practical matters. 'How long is it since you saw this friend of your
father's, Lucien?'

'Maybe two or three years,' he said. 'When his wife
died I attended her funeral; but at one time I spent a
great deal of time visiting the Corsis. They were good
friends to me when I came to Corsica on my own for the
first time to begin as a wine-grower, twelve years ago.
But——' another shrug both made excuses and regretted
the lapse of an old friendship, 'we are both busy men.
My father and Maurice exchange greetings, but Papa
does not travel so much now and it is not the same to
write letters, eh?' He smiled and nodded, dismissing
regrets in favour of the coming visit. 'But you will like
Maurice, Troy, and it will be good to see an old friend
once more.'

Driving on a road that traversed the flank of the
mountain in breathtaking twists and turns, they seemed
at times to be suspended above the rest of the world,
among the rugged mountain scenery yet within sight
now of a small town in the valley below, and of the
glittering blue ocean off to their left.

The town sprawled out across the valley, then outward to the coast, the pale stone buildings blending in perfectly with their surroundings, and sitting contentedly in the warm spring sunshine. Three and four-storey houses, square-towered churches with domed tops and the almost inevitable grim, squat Genoese fortress, a relic of the unhappy past, dominating the hillside above the town; Troy could guess it was their destination, even before Lucien pointed it out.

'There! There is Benecollocare, Troy,' he said, and she craned forward to get a better view.

It had a hazy and slightly dreamlike quality seen at this distance and from the high road, but it looked very pretty and tranquil and an ideal place in which to spend a holiday. Whether it would come up to expectations at ground level remained to be seen, but she liked what she saw so far. 'It looks quite small,' she remarked, and Lucien smiled.

'There are no huge towns and cities on Corsica, *cara mia*,' he reminded her. 'Not such as you are accustomed to elsewhere, the island is very small. But soon I think Benecollocare will begin to grow now that it has caught the eyes of the tourist.'

In two minds whether or not the prospect was pleasing, Troy watched the little town grow and become distinct as they got closer and she saw nothing that changed her first impression as yet. 'Is your friend in the tourist business, Lucien?' she asked, and he spared a moment from negotiating the quite perilous drop on one side of them, to glance at her.

'He was once a farmer in Nemio, but——' A resigned shrug conveyed his meaning perfectly. 'Like so many others Maurice was forced by conditions to make a choice. But unlike Papa and many others he did not emigrate, instead he opened a small hotel and fortunately it profited by the new interest in Corsica as a tourist spot. He now has a larger hotel, and when I saw him last he was beginning to see his reward.'

'Good for him!'

Troy's response was rather vague because she was giving most of her attention to their immediate surroundings. As yet the streets they drove through were narrow, and tall houses hemmed them in on both sides, their tiers of shuttered windows half open, like sleepy eyes in the sunshine.

Façades were patched and eroded by time and weather, and the occasional wrought iron balcony that overhung the street was more reminiscent of the East than part of France. Here and there a solitary tree showed itself above a wall, somehow clinging to life among the arid streets and softening crumbling walls with its uneasy, fluttering shadows.

Then almost abruptly the streets began to widen and the rows of buildings became more regular; the trees, no longer fighting for existence, but set tidily among concrete lamp-posts, their shadows neat and orderly. There were hotels and shops as well as houses and a different kind of people too; people who moved more hurriedly and with more purpose, where the modern world encroached upon the ancient *citadelle* and opened it up.

Lucien brought the car to a halt in front of a small three-storey hotel that opened directly off the street as so many of the buildings did. But the first impression was of a family home rather than the entrance to an hotel, and almost as soon as they walked in through the door a man came forward to greet them.

He was short and plump and grey-haired with a brown weatherbeaten face that sported a luxuriant moustache, and he was smiling; two hands outstretched in recognition and welcome. 'Lucien!'

There followed a spate of words that tumbled joyously over one another like a lyrical waterfall, and Lucien's hand was pumped up and down enthusiastically all the while. Both visitor and host did their share of talking, but Lucien was perhaps a little less wildly garrulous than the older man, and after a moment or two he turned and put a hand on Troy's arm, drawing her forward.

'Maurice, my friend, do you still remember your English?'

For a second only the man's small bright eyes looked at him curiously, then he evidently followed his meaning and nodded energetically. 'But of course!' he said.

'The young lady speaks neither Corse nor French,' Lucien explained before he introduced her. 'I should like you to meet Miss Troy Liskard from England, Maurice. Troy, this is a very good friend, Monsieur Maurice Corsi. And please,' he added with a gleam of laughter in his black eyes, 'do not imagine that he will not understand you—Maurice is very fluent in English, unless he has forgotten all he was taught!'

The compliment obviously pleased the little man and he beamed his pleasure as he extended a hand in welcome, while Troy chose to disregard the reference to her first gaffe regarding Lucien's English. He could seldom resist reminding her of her initial impression of him, although Troy always did her best not to rise to the bait, as now.

'I am most pleased to welcome you, Mademoiselle Liskard,' her host assured her, and bobbed a brief bow over her hand. 'As you see I have not forgotten my English!'

'Your English is perfect, Monsieur Corsi!'

Once more a beam of gratification illuminated the brown face, and he bobbed his head. '*Merci, mademoiselle; merci beaucoup!* But come, it is not fitting that friends should be kept standing in the foyer; please to come through to my rooms. Mademoiselle—Lucien!'

With extravagant gestures of his hands and arms he invited them to follow him into his living quarters, and he saw them comfortably seated in armchairs before offering them wine. Eyeing it in the glass, he gave Lucien a bright challenging smile. 'You recognise your own vintage, eh, Lucien?'

Lucien looked so completely at ease, leaning back in the big armchair, one leg crossed over the other, and he acknowledged the compliment to his wine with a raised brow and a half-smile as he held up his glass. 'You could not do better, Maurice—*à votre santé!*'

Maurice Corsi replied to the toast with a nod. '*A la vôtre, mon ami!* Mademoiselle!'

Troy made her own silent toast and sampled the wine cautiously, for more than once her grandfather had commented on the potency of Corsican wines. This was no ordinary country wine, however, she realised it as soon as she took her first sip, and she looked across at Lucien with a hint of surprise that seemed to amuse him.

'You like it, Troy?' he asked, and she nodded, trying to remember the last time she had had it.

It was a clear, delicate rose pink and the taste was slightly scented, as if it took its bouquet from the massed perfumes of the maquis that surrounded the vineyards. She took another sip and it came to her then where she had had it before; she had been served the same wine when she dined with Lucien on her first evening in Nemio. Only then she had not realised it was his own produce.

'It's very good indeed,' she told him, and was quite unconscious of the slight lift of her chin when she looked at him. 'I remember having it before, don't I?'

'Indeed you have!' Lucien's black eyes gleamed in that deep and infinitely disturbing way that usually made her so uneasy, but in this instance it seemed merely to heighten her appreciation of the wine she was drinking. Both gave her the same warm glowing sense of well-being. 'You have a good memory, Troy, I must see that you have a bottle for your own use when we return!'

'I'm not normally a wine drinker, but I'll hold you to that!'

Lucien smiled, murmured something in Italian, then turned his attention once more to Maurice Corsi. 'How is the hotel business, Maurice? You have no regrets that you gave up farming to become an *hôtelier*?'

'None at all, my friend!' The man's small bright eyes gleamed with amusement as he regarded him a second before he spoke. 'And you, Lucien—you have no regrets that you gave up the pleasures of *le galant* to become a wine-grower?'

'None at all,' Lucien assured him, sipping from his glass. 'And it is many years since I was what Troy's countrymen would call a playboy, *hein*?' Clearly it was also an image he was anxious to live down, for having hastily dismissed the subject he hastened on with his original enquiry. 'You seem to have a thriving business here,' he told his host with a smile. 'Your hotel has the look of—class!'

A shrug of Maurice Corsi's plump shoulders implied satisfaction. 'At the moment there are spare rooms, of course, it is early in the year, but later——' The spread of his hands suggested an endless succession of summer visitors, and he nodded his head, his lower lip pursed. 'Things go well; *très bien, merci*!'

Turning his wine glass slowly in his hands while he watched the contents gleam silkily in the light, Lucien did not look up when he spoke. 'How is Cécile?' he asked.

'Ah!' Once more their host's expression showed the assumed carelessness of satisfaction, the weatherbeaten face creased in a broad smile. 'She is well and happy, Lucien, *merci*! You knew that she had married?'

'I heard.' Lucien acknowledged it briefly and Troy thought she detected a hint of reserve in his manner, but that could simply have been her imagination. 'Another schoolteacher, I understand? You must be very pleased, Maurice?'

'*Mais oui!*' Maurice looked across at Troy and smiled

as he went on to explain. 'Cécile is my daughter, Mademoiselle Liskard, and she became a schoolteacher. To do this she must go to the mainland, you understand, for the training.' The mainland was the way most Corsicans referred to France, Troy knew, and she nodded her understanding. 'One year ago,' Maurice went on, 'she tells me that she is to be married—just like so! I am taken by surprise, but she is almost thirty years and my only child, so naturally I am delighted. Like all men I wish one day to be a *grandpère*!'

'You must be very proud of her, *monsieur*.' He had reminded her of one of Lucien's reasons for bringing her there, but it was not her place to raise the matter of her own grandfather, Troy felt. All the same she glanced at Lucien to see if he was going to remember in his own time.

'I am most certainly proud,' Maurice agreed, but his eyes too turned in Lucien's direction. 'I had hoped——' He shrugged his shoulders, apparently in resignation, and smiled again. 'But her husband is a good man and they are suited.'

Quite clearly Maurice Corsi had had someone else in mind as a son-in-law, but Troy did not look at Lucien to see if he showed any of the same signs of disappointment at the way things had worked out. Instead she asked further after their host's daughter. 'What subject does your daughter teach, Monsieur Corsi?'

'English Literature, *mademoiselle*!' His pride was touching, and Troy smiled in sympathy with it. 'It was Cécile who taught her *papa* to speak English, and also my friend Lucien here, eh, *mon brave*?'

'She was an excellent teacher,' Lucien agreed with a smile, and caught Troy's eye briefly.

'You should know best, my friend!' Maurice poured them all more wine and he was obviously enjoying himself immensely; laughing until his round weathered face was suffused with colour and his small dark eyes twinkled wickedly with meaning. 'The hours and hours that you spent learning English from Cécile, my friend, you should be *le professeur*! But then it is not only English that you learn together, eh?' He roared with merriment at his jest, and Lucien too was laughing though with less exuberance, both shaking their heads over shared reminiscences.

'We were young,' Lucien said, as if explanation was needed, and Troy recalled that Pietro had told her his uncle had not learned his English in the schoolroom. Obviously he had spoken the truth, but Troy could not help speculating just how much time had been spent learning English in the company of Cécile Corsi, and how much on less academic subjects.

The speculation did not last very long, for Maurice remembered his duties as a host and as he reached for the wine bottle once more he recalled himself. 'But I have not enquired of your *papa*, Lucien, and your sister, your mother—they are all well, I hope?'

'All very well, *merci*, Maurice.' Lucien took another sip of his wine before confiding anything further, and then he did so with an almost careless air. 'Pietro is staying with me at the moment; Bianca's elder son.'

'Oh?' Obviously the fact aroused his host's curiosity, and his bright inquisitive eyes briefly glanced at Troy. 'It is a—holiday?'

Lucien shook his head, both in answer to the question and to the offer of more wine. 'Not officially,' he said. 'Bianca is coming over very soon to see him and to settle the matter.'

Maurice looked sympathetic, nodding his head as if he understood well the problems of bringing up a family. 'Trouble?' he enquired, but Lucien shook his head.

'Nothing that cannot be settled,' he declared with such firmness that Troy gave him a reproachful look, one of which he was apparently unaware. She found it hard to believe that he was as resolutely indifferent to Pietro's future as he appered to be. 'On the matter of families, Maurice,' he went on, glancing at Troy from the corner of his eye as he spoke. 'It was not entirely on my own behalf that I came to see you after so long, but for Mademoiselle Liskard's sake.'

Once more the small dark eyes gleamed with curiosity when they settled on Troy, and a rumbling laugh shook his rotund body. 'I would suppose you to do much for Mademoiselle Liskard's sake, *mon brave*!'

A slight smile ackowledged the implication, but obviously Lucien was above being embarrassed by it. 'I wished to ask if you ever knew someone called——' He glanced once more at Troy to confirm the name and she supplied it hastily.

'Robert Milleaux, Monsieur Corsi. Did you ever know someone called Robert Milleaux?'

'Milleaux.' He repeated the name giving it a French sound and frowning over it for a moment, so that Troy provided a description to aid his memory, learning forward in her chair as she did so.

'He was a tall man, and dark, going grey, with blue eyes and very thin face, and he was a keen naturalist. He used to spend a lot of time here, when he was a boy and later, after he was married, though not so much in the last twenty years or so, perhaps.'

'Ah, *oui*!' Obviously something struck him as familair, for Maurice's expressive features were wreathed in smiles and he was using his hands extravagantly. 'The man who loved the maquis?' Obviously her grandfather's penchant for spending whole days simply noting the rich variety of plant life that his hosts took for granted had been a source of amusement. 'A Frenchman, is he not, *mademoiselle*? And he married a beautiful English girl who—Ah!' He flicked his eyes in Lucien's direction, then back to Troy once more, and it seemed to Troy that he was being more cautious suddenly. 'You know him, this Monsieur Milleaux, *mademoiselle*?'

'I knew him very well,' Troy told him, her voice well under control. 'He was my grandfather, Monsieur Corsi; he died last year.'

'*Je regrette beaucoup, mademoiselle!*'

Troy acknowledged his sympathy almost absently because something in his manner puzzled her, and she thought Lucien had noticed it too. 'Did you know him, Monsieur Corsi? Did you know my grandfather?'

'No, *mademoiselle*, I regret that I did not. I knew—of him, you understand, that is all.' Once more he gave Lucien a brief and meaningful look, but this time Lucien took up the matter and questioned him about it.

'Did my father know Monsieur Milleaux, Maurice?'

The little man hesitated, switching his uneasy glance between them for several moments before he replied. Then he spread his hands wide, almost in appeal, and shrugged. 'It was rumour only, *mon ami*, and after all these years——'

Lucien's black eyes sought Troy's opinion, and she nodded her agreement practically without realising she did so, anxious to know what it was that made Maurice Corsi so reluctant to answer. 'Let us have the rumour, Maurice, *s'il vous plaît*; both Mademoiselle and myself are too interested now to be satisfied with less than the whole story.'

Troy had no idea what she expected, but it was obvious that Maurice Corsi did not relish repeating old gossip, no matter how vague. In the circumstances he saw himself with little option, however, and once more a shrug recognised the fact. Fortified with more wine, he leaned back in his chair and addressed himself primarily to Lucien initially.

'There was no confirmation, you understand, none at all, but it was said in the village that Alexandre Gaffori had—eyes for the pretty English wife of the visitor, Robert Milleaux. It was said that she was the reason he left Corsica to go to Italy, but—who knows for sure?'

Troy was too startled by the turn of events to say anything at the moment, but Lucien was obviously intrigued, and he looked across at her with raised brows and a trace of irony in his smile. 'So,' he said softly, 'we have a secret romance, eh?'

'No, no, my friend!' Maurice denied hastily, using his hands to refute the idea. 'There was never any romance; the lady was married and Alexandre was an honourable man! No, no—no romance, most certainly no romance!'

'You seem so very certain of it, Maurice,' Lucien said, and his eyes narrowed slightly. 'Did he confide in you? You were his friend, did he confide his love for the English girl?'

'No, Lucien, he did not!' The little man drew himself up and looked at him gravely, obviously disturbed to realise he could have raised a very discomfiting ghost. 'I knew nothing but what I heard in the cafés, and you will know how unreliable such gossip can be, my friend.'

Lucien nodded, as if he was bound to admit the extravagance of the talk the men exchanged over their wine, but he must know too, as Troy did, that there was seldom smoke without fire. 'It is so very—intriguing, Maurice, that is all,' he consoled the hotelier, and smiled at him wryly. 'I am simply intrigued to realise that my *papa* has the soul of a romantic when I have always thought of him as the most practical man I know! It is refreshing to learn new aspects of one's parents, do you not agree, Troy?'

'I suppose so,' Troy allowed, still rather bemused. 'But your father must have been—must be a very honest man to have behaved as he did. An honourable man, as Monsieur Corsi says.'

'And a wise one as it turned out,' Lucien remarked with a touch of dryness. 'Had he not left for Italy he might still be a shepherd in the mountains instead of a wealthy wine-grower!'

'Lucien——' Maurice was looking at him with a trace

of anxiety. 'You will be discreet, my friend, eh? You will say nothing of this matter to your *papa*?'

'Of course not!' The bold black eyes challenged anyone to disbelieve him. Obviously reassured, Maurice visibly relaxed, and Lucien turned his attention again to Troy, a lingering warmth in his eyes. 'It is not difficult to imagine the young Madame Milleaux was very lovely,' he said in the voice that always stirred something in her senses. 'How could anyone blame him, especially his son?'

Maurice Corsi was quick to recover and he laughed, winking broadly at his visitor. 'Like her granddaughter, eh, *mon brave*?' he asked.

'I would think very much like her granddaughter,' Lucien agreed, and smiled when he noted Troy's swift flush of colour. *'Bellissima!'* he added softly.

They drove home through the cool shadows of late afternoon, and Troy felt a strange sense of tranquillity as she watched the dying daylight lend new expressions to the dark rugged features of the man beside her. Lucien had been revealed to her today as he never had before, and she felt closer to him somehow, and not only because his father was rumoured to have loved her grandmother in vain. She made up her mind never to mention that matter again.

Instead she offered him formal thanks in a voice that was unconsciously a little reserved because she found him a rather disturbing companion when she allowed herself to think about it. 'I'm very grateful to you for taking me to see your friend,' she said, and Lucien turned his head for a moment when he recognised the formality of her manner.

'You enjoyed your visit?'

'Very much so, thank you, Lucien.' She left matters there for a second or two, then took advantage of the shadowy light that disguised her face to some extent, and raised a matter that had been on her mind almost as much as her grandmother's fascination for Gaffori senior. 'And I now know where you learned to speak such perfect English.' He said nothing, so she pressed on. 'Mademoiselle Corsi must be a very good teacher.'

'Madame Giran,' Lucian corrected her quietly, and without confirming how good an instructor she had been. 'You forget she is now married!'

'And she was pretty too, no doubt.'

'Very pretty,' he agreed, and Troy realised he was smiling.

Inexplicably irritated by the fact, she was unable to resist further comment, and she looked straight ahead at the narrow road between tall straight pines while she spoke. 'Pietro was right then, when he said you didn't learn your English in the schoolroom, though you *did* learn it from a schoolteacher. But he probably didn't know that!'

Lucien changed gear and drove the car very carefully round a bend that marked the first thinning of the forest before it gave way to open mountainside and the more familiar scene she was used to. She thought he raised a brow briefly before he answered, as if the tone of her voice surprised him, but he did not turn his head.

'Pietro says far too much about matters that do not concern him,' he observed coolly, and Troy felt the colour in her cheeks at the unmistakable hint, as she saw it.

'Then I suppose the same ruling applies to me,' she said in a voice that was not quite steady although she tried to control it. 'I'm sorry I've been talking about things that don't concern me!'

He half turned his head and for a second only the black eyes looked directly into hers, deep as jet in the shadow of thick lashes and the diminishing light of evening. 'You do not have to apologise for anything,' he told her, and a glimpse of white showed her that he was close to smiling. 'Nor is there need for you to sound so—angry, Troy. This outing was intended to please you, not to upset you.'

'I'm not upset!'

In the distance and coming closer every minute, Nemio straggled down the mountainside, with La Casa Antica sitting like a benign goddess on the highest terrace above the rest of the village. Turning briefly once more, Lucien smiled and caught her eye, his own glowing blackly in his strong, brigand's face.

'Then smile, *cara mia*, eh?' he said, and Troy did so instinctively.

CHAPTER SIX

TROY had allowed herself to be persuaded. It was all too easy to be persuaded when Pietro assumed the ill-used look that he was so adept at. But if she was quite honest, she could see Lucien's point of view when he refused to allow his expensive and high-powered car to be driven on mountain roads by someone as flamboyantly careless as Pietro.

Troy was driving into Dentreau to buy another supply of groceries, so she was not putting herself out all, and she was quite happy to have Pietro along, purely for the ride, so he said. He was a lively companion and he had felt it keenly, being left behind when she drove to Benecollocare with Lucien a couple of days ago. In some way, she felt, this might make up for it.

So far she had heard nothing more about the telephone call he had stayed behind to take on Lucien's behalf, but she had little doubt that sooner or later he would enlighten her; Pietro was given to confidences. She could not imagine why he chose to be picked up part way along the track through the vineyard, but that was what he had said he wanted to do, and she saw him there as she bumped along over the tractor ridges. Darkly handsome in navy slacks and a white sports shirt and thumbing a lift in the manner of a hitch-hiker, he glanced swiftly over his shoulder before sliding into the seat beside her.

Troy looked at him curiously. 'I thought you might have changed your mind about coming,' she remarked, and Pietro grinned disarmingly.

'But of course I haven't,' he told her, adding with stunning frankness, 'I just did not want Lucien to see me leaving with you, that's all.'

To Troy his meaning was in little doubt and she unconsciously turned her head to look at him briefly just before she turned her little car out on to the road. 'I hardly think Lucien is likely to object to you driving into Dentreau with me,' she told him, then suddenly suspected another reason for his secretiveness. 'Unless you're supposed to be doing something for Lucien, are you, Pietro? You're not playing truant, are you?'

He was familiar enough from his English schooldays with the term truant to take exception to it, and he frowned in a way that gave his young face an incredible likeness to his uncle. 'I am not a schoolboy any more, Troy, I do not have to play truant! It is simply that— well, I prefer that Lucien does not know that I have come with you.'

'Oh, I see.'

Troy said nothing further for fear of evoking fresh comment on her own situation with Lucien; it was not a matter she cared to discuss and especially with Pietro. Instead she took her time, following the same steep road she had driven along the day she arrived in Nemio, this time going downward towards the more fertile valley.

Dentreau was smaller than Benecollocare, but it provided what she needed and it had a good open-air market selling fresh, local grown fruit and vegetables. She had only to mention Madame Coron's name to be shown the courtesy reserved for friends and special customers. What Pietro intended doing with himself while she was shopping, she had no idea, for he was hardly likely to be interested in buying provisions.

He was young, but he was old enough and near enough to her own age for his attentions to be appreciated, and he was certainly good-looking and very Latin in his flattery. She could hardly fault him as an escort and he was almost overwhelmingly anxious to please, but she had not anticipated him offering to carry her heavier purchases. He drew the line at being seen with a basket of vegetables, however, and eventually Troy carried it herself, slung from her arm in the best peasant tradition, according to Pietro.

She chose her cheese with care. Nearly a month of Madame Coron's tuition had taught her what to look for, and she particularly liked the mildness of *basteli-caccia*, choosing that as well as a *brocciu* for adding with fresh mint to her favourite omelette. Her culinary skills, she realised with a secret smile, were improving by leaps and bounds and mostly in regional dishes passed on to her by Lucien's housekeeper.

The market always fascinated her and she could have spent much longer looking around at the rainbow piles of fruit and vegetables, at the staggering variety of fish that the nearby ocean provided for the taking. She always bought fruit and found the flavour so much richer when oranges had not been long off the trees. But to Pietro the interest was soon gone and he was impatient to be away.

'You have finished shopping?' he asked as they piled her purchases into the boot of her car, and Troy nodded, unable to resist a smile.

'Actually I was rather surprised you came shopping with me,' she told him. 'I hadn't seen you as domesticated, Pietro, but I was very glad of your help carrying the things.'

His smile was vaguely sheepish and he hunched his shoulders briefly in the inevitable shrug. 'I am not domesticated,' he denied. 'I wished to be with you, Troy, as I told you, and if helping you with your marketing was the only way I could do that then——' Another shrug accompanied a sideways glance. 'I must come and carry your shopping for you.'

Troy could not rid herself of the suspicion that there was some other reason behind his desire to be with her this morning, but she could think of none but the one he claimed at the moment, and that should be flattering enough for anyone. 'Well, I'm grateful, whatever your reason for coming,' she said, and glanced at him from the corner of her eye as she closed the boot of the car and locked it.

Pietro's dark eyes had that irresistible look of appeal once more, and she was almost sure she knew what his next suggestion was going to be. She had anticipated it from the moment they started out and she had no intention of turning it down. Leaning his face closer as they stood beside the car, he linked his arm through hers.

'We will have lunch in Dentreau, eh, Troy?'

'Yes, please!' She laughed at his blink of surprise when her prompt reply put him at a loss for a second. 'I've never had lunch here before,' she told him, 'and I was hoping you'd ask me; thank you, Pietro.'

He looked so inordinately pleased that Troy was touched without quite knowing why at first. Pietro, she thought with sudden insight, was much more sensitive about his present situation than he appeared to be on the surface, and he took her agreeing to have lunch with him as a sign of approval. Taking her arm, he drew her along the narrow street and around a corner into another, slightly wider and with a small restaurant half way along its length.

Its façade was not impressive, but Troy had visited France often enough to recognise that the proof of a restaurant is in its fare, not its exterior, and she willingly accompanied him inside and sat at one of the small tables. 'It is not luxury,' Pietro apologised as he took his seat facing her, 'but it is good, I can promise you that, Troy.'

'And not too expensive, I hope,' she said, smoothing over the practicality of the words with a smile. 'I don't imagine you're very well off at the moment, Pietro, and I don't want to be the means of making things even worse.'

'Don't worry,' he assured her, and so swiftly avoided her eyes when he said it that Troy frowned at him curiously for a moment. 'What will you have?'

He offered her the menu, but she indicated that she would rather he chose, while she sat considering the street outside. His French, she noticed absently, was good enough though not as fluently confident as Lucien's. She had no way of knowing just how much money he had managed to bring out of Italy with him, or if Lucien had supplemented his supply, but in any case she did not want to be the means of him spending too much or Bianco Gerolamo, when she eventually came on the scene, might get quite the wrong idea about her.

In fact the fare was good but fairly everyday by Corsican standards, catering for the local market people rather than visitors as Benecollocare did, and Troy was by now well enough accustomed to the different tastes of the Corsican palate not to be shocked to see roast blackbird on the menu. Probably because he realised she would draw the line at actually eating them, Pietro ordered their simple vegetable and herb soup to be followed by roast kid with a variety of vegetables, finishing with *fiadonu*, a kind of fritter made from chestnuts.

The wine was a local one, though not of the quality that Maurice Corsi had offered her and Lucien, a bottle of which now stood part empty on her kitchen shelf to be finished with her evening meal. But it was good if rather rough, and stronger than she had tried so far, so that she felt remarkably bright as she sipped it and looked across the empty dishes at Pietro.

'You have enjoyed it?' he asked, but she thought he knew the answer well enough and she smiled and nodded her head.

'Very much, thank you, it was delicious! But I'm glad you didn't order the roast blackbird for me, Pietro—I don't think I could have faced that!'

Pietro grinned and his dark eyes were brighter than

ever after having consumed most of the wine. 'I know how sentimental you English are about birds,' he teased. 'Although why you should be so much more sentimental about a bird than a very small baby goat I cannot imagine, but you enjoyed the kid, yes?'

'Yes, I did,' Troy agreed, but pouted her mouth reproachfully as she did so. 'But I'd rather you didn't remind me of that, Pietro, or you'll ruin my enjoyment if you go on.'

'Then I will not go on!' He was laughing at her as he shook his head then, with unaccustomed boldness, he reached over and took her hand, fondling her fingers while he talked and looking at her in a half-teasing way that was rather reminiscent of his uncle. 'You are very lovely, Troy, and I wish——' He shrugged, laughed lightly and shook his head, then let go of her hand. 'I will not go too far,' he declared with mock seriousness, 'for fear of arousing Lucien's wrath—that I cannot afford to do at the moment!'

Discomfited as always by the allusion, Troy frowned at him. 'I don't see why you have to assume that Lucien will say or do anything about it,' she told him. 'I rent my cottage from him, that's all, Pietro; and that *is* all!' She disliked the smile that glittered in his dark eyes and brought so many disturbing thoughts to mind, and it was with the idea of turning the tables that she changed the subject. 'I'd take wagers that you've got a girl-friend in Rome, haven't you?' she asked, confident of the answer.

'Of course!'

His smile was unabashed and he toyed with the stem of his wine glass but made no attempt to avoid her eyes. 'Don't you miss her?' she asked, and his eyes gleamed with laughter as he leaned across the table towards her.

'Which one?' he asked. 'Maria, Gabriella, Lucia— which one, Troy?'

'I see!' Troy conceded his ability to charm her sex and guessed he was not at all unwilling to discuss his conquests if she but gave him half a chance. 'Well, one of them must be missing you.'

'They all will be,' he boasted matter-of-factly, and she could not resist a smile at such unshakeable confidence. 'I do not have just one girl, Troy, I have many, and I do not become too serious with anyone. You have the saying in England, do you not, that there is safety in numbers?'

'We also have another saying,' Troy retorted swiftly. 'Love 'em and leave 'em—though it's not a very sympathetic reputation to get!'

'Sympathetic?' Obviously it was a use of the word he had not come across before, for all his fluency in English, and he quizzed her with his dark eyes across the table. 'Why do I need sympathy, Troy?'

'I didn't say you did,' Troy told him, shrugging off the idea of explaining. 'It doesn't matter, Pietro, it's just a figure of speech.'

But he had followed the general gist of her meaning, obviously, for he was looking at her with a directness that was slightly discomfiting in the circumstances. 'Do you take it seriously every time a man—looks at you, Troy?'

'No, of course I don't!' She was aware as she hastily denied it of how loud his voice seemed in the small restaurant and she glanced around her uneasily before attempting to let him know it. 'Pietro, it's very quiet in here and——'

'Then I do not see the difference between you and me,' Pietro declared, ignoring her attempts to keep their conversation private. 'Do you take Lucien seriously when he flirts with you? Do you call Lucien—love them and leave them, hah?'

Troy glanced uneasily around once more, then shook her head. 'Please, Pietro, this is neither the time nor the place to talk about Lucien! And anyway, that's not the same thing at all.'

He looked at her with his dark eyes gleaming and she knew there was little chance of his giving up the debate until he had satisfied himself he was right in his argument. 'Because Lucien is older? Is that what you mean by not the same thing, Troy? Eh?'

He had somehow become much more Italian in the last few moments and much more excitable, but Troy tried at last to keep her side of the conversation at a reasonable level. 'I don't necessarily mean that, Pietro,' she said, her fingers tight around the stem of her glass. 'Now can we please leave the subject of Lucien?'

'By all means,' he conceded obligingly, 'if that is what you want to do. I find you a much more intriguing subject for discussion anyway. Tell me about yourself, Troy. Do you have brothers or sisters?'

Anything was better than the disturbing subject of Lucien and she was nothing loath to talk about herself if that was what he wanted. Apparently he was not a smoker, or if he was he did not smoke after their meal, and it served again to remind her of how young he was. Little more than a schoolboy still, until he had absconded from his school in a bid for independence. He would find it difficult to understand what it was like being an only child too, she guessed, coming as he did from a fairly large family.

'I'm an only one,' she told him, and his expression confirmed her guess.

'Do you not find it very lonely?' he asked. 'With no other children in the family?'

Troy had never found it so and she shook her head. 'I have cousins, and school friends, some of whom I still keep in touch with. I've never noticed I was lonely.'

'You have travelled?'

'Not as much as you have,' she smiled, remembering his diplomatic background. 'But I've been to a couple of places.'

'But you have never been to Corsica before. Lucien

told me that you were strange to the island,' he added with a smile. 'I was interested and Lucien never minds talking about you, although I do not think he knows very much about you, does he, Troy?'

They were back on the inevitable subject of Lucien, Troy realised with a sigh, and answered him with a certain air of resignation which he almost certainly noticed. 'I don't go around telling everyone my life story,' she said, and pulled a face before naming the exception. 'Unless someone asks me, as you did, of course.'

He made no apology for his curiosity, but reached for her hand again, folding his slim boy's fingers over hers firmly. 'I wish to know all about you,' he declared. 'And you surely do not mind me asking, do you, Troy?' He scarcely waited for the brief shake of her head before pressing on with his quiz. 'Have you ever been to Italy?'

'Only once,' she admitted. 'I'd love to go again some time, I thought it was a wonderful country; and I've been to France three or four times on holiday, though I never managed to learn to speak very much French, even then.'

'So Lucien said.'

Troy frowned without realising she did it. 'You and Lucien seem to have been discussing me a lot lately,' she said. 'I can't imagine why you find me such an absorbing topic, with so much going on that should concern you far more than I do.'

In other circumstances Pietro's answer might have amused her, but she was a little too distracted at the moment to see the humour of it. 'Men always discuss beautiful women they admire,' he told her with an air of nonchalance that would have done credit to his uncle. 'You're not thinking of going back to England yet, are you, Troy? You do like it here?'

'It's beautiful, even more beautiful than I expected from all that Grandpère told me about it.' She could say that without reservation. 'He loved it here and I always wanted to come and see it for myself; now that I have I can't think why I waited so long.'

'And now you will stay?'

'For a while at least; until I finish Grandpère Milleaux's book anyway. Though that could be a lot longer than I first planned!'

'Perhaps forever?' Pietro suggested with a smile that somehow she found oddly discomfiting, and she shook her head.

'Oh, I don't know about that; forever's a pretty long time!'

Pietro's dark eyes sparkled with mischief and he leaned further across the table towards her, holding her hand tightly in his. 'But suppose you met someone you— liked very specially, Troy? Someone you might even wish to marry, perhaps?'

Freeing her hand wasn't easy, but Troy achieved it with a minimum of fuss and only wished it was as easy to do something about the colour that suddenly warmed her cheeks to a flushed pink. Gathering up her handbag from the empty chair beside her, she made it obvious that she was ready to leave, whether or not Pietro was.

'I've nothing at all like that in mind, Pietro!' she told him in a voice she tried desperately to steady. 'I'm not here looking for romance or marriage or anything else like that; I'm here to complete my grandfather's book, and that's all!'

Laughter glittered darkly in his eyes and he was shaking his head, his mouth pursed in apparent disappointment. 'Not even a little affair to pass the time, Troy?'

'No!'

When the waiter brought their bill, Pietro was still smiling broadly, as if the whole situation amused him enormously, and even while he was paying the man he shook his head slowly, as if in regret. 'That is a pity,' he said with mock sadness. 'It would have made it so much more exciting, *no*?'

'For you? Pietro——'

'For *some*one,' Pietro said, and laughed as the man walked off with a generous tip.

Troy did her best to appear composed by firmly quelling an all too easily remembered few moments on a mountainside with Lucien. His arms wrapped tightly around her and his body pressing her close to the ground while some indiscriminate Corsican shepherd let off a rifle at them under the mistaken impression that he was shooting at a wild dog. Suppose she did meet someone she wanted to marry—? Shaking her head firmly, she got up and walked away from the table with her head in the air and a glint of determination in her blue eyes. She was there to finish Grandpère's book and that was all— just as she told Pietro. Only she thought Pietro was not altogether convinced.

When they arrived back at the cottage Pietro was very helpful in taking the shopping from the car into the cottage for her, and she was a little surprised to see him apply himself so diligently to such a mundane task. The reason for it was explained when she turned from taking the last few packages from the back of the car and saw Lucien coming across the yard with the obvious intention of joining her.

'Hello, Lucien!'

She smiled automatically, but something about his expression banished the smile almost as soon as it formed, and she glanced at Pietro who emerged from the cottage at exactly the same moment. He saw his uncle, faltered in his step for a second, then thrust his hands into the pockets of his slacks in an unmistakably defiant gesture that puzzled Troy.

'So,' Lucien said without preliminary, 'you decide not to stay and welcome your *mamma* when she comes to see you, eh?' Pietro sent her a swift uneasy glance but said nothing yet, and Lucien went on in a deep voice that was vibrant with anger. It was clear that what he had to say he would much rather have said in Italian, and refrained from doing so only from courtesy to Troy. 'Nor did you think it necessary to let me or anyone else know where you were going or even that you were going anywhere at all! *Dio mio, Pietro,* I could——' He broke off quickly, shaking his head.

Pietro had obviously hoped to delay the inevitable scene until he was in the house and he had put off that moment as long as possible; also he did not relish being reprimanded in front of Troy. In the circumstances she could feel a certain amount of sympathy for both of them, but she found it oddly disturbing to see Lucien so angry, and she could do nothing about leaving them to their quarrel because Lucien's tall lean figure blocked her way.

'And you still seek to encourage him, Troy!'

Being drawn so unexpectedly into the scene Troy blinked at him in blank surprise for a moment. Apparently because Pietro chose to be a silent culprit and say nothing, Lucien sought another and more responsive opponent. But Troy had no intention of taking blame for anything that was not her doing and she coloured furiously, her hands curled tightly over the packages she held, while she glared at him.

'I knew nothing about your sister arriving today,' she told him in a slightly breathless voice. 'Your family affairs don't concern me, Lucien, you know that! I didn't know about his mother, and when Pietro asked if he could come with me into Dentreau I saw no valid reason to refuse!'

Lucien's black eyes surveyed her for a moment as if he tried to make up his mind whether or not she was telling him the truth. 'He did not tell you *why* he wished to go with you?' he asked, and Troy shook her head firmly.

'Being a woman I was conceited enough to believe

him when he said he just wanted to be with me!' she told him, her chin angled in a way he could not possibly mistake; and she noticed a hint of movement at one corner of his mouth that decided her against confessing her own earlier suspicions.

He shook his head slowly and the smile grew into something more certain. 'Another wrong end of the stick?' he suggested, and the pitch of his voice had dropped a full octave.

Despairing of her own responsive senses, Troy nodded. 'It seems like it,' she said, 'and it isn't me who has hold of it this time! I had no idea that Pietro was expecting his mother to arrive today.' She looked up swiftly and caught his eye, her cheeks still flushed with colour, but defiantly honest. 'I don't know how I'd have answered him if I had known,' she told him, and Lucien smiled again.

'So honest, Troy, eh?' He glanced into the back of the car. 'Is that the last of your shopping? If so perhaps you will like to come and meet Bianca when you have done whatever you have to do.'

He had a hand on Pietro's shoulder, she noticed a little dazedly, and his black eyes had a glimpse of the same irresistible appeal that made Pietro so hard to refuse as he looked down at her, so that she almost accepted the invitation without stopping to think. Only then she reminded herself that it was a completely family affair, and she did not want to become involved in it.

It almost seemed as if Lucien anticipated her objection, for he shook his head and placed his other hand on her shoulder, his strong fingers curved firmly into her flesh. 'You need not fear that you will become involved in anything, Troy, there will be no—confrontation for the moment. My sister has brought a friend with her from Italy—Signora Arturo; it is all very informal.'

Troy was aware from the corner of her eye of Pietro's

reaction to the other visitor's name, and she glanced at him curiously. His lips were pursed in a silent whistle and there was a bright speculative gleam in his eyes. Then he flicked his dark brows and swivelled his eyes in Lucien's direction with such obvious meaning that it was impossible for Troy not to get the message. Signora Arturo was evidently another part of Lucien's past, like Cécile Corsi.

Catching sight of him, Lucien frowned. 'You had best go and see your *mamma, ragazzo mio!*' he told him. 'I will follow in a few moments when I have had a word with Troy.'

Pietro's shrug was resigned and so far, Troy realised, he had not said a word since his uncle's arrival, though she doubted if he was quite as subdued as he might appear. Looking up into Lucien's dark implacable features once more, she wondered what he would do if it came to Pietro's wishes being completely disregarded where his future was concerned. In her heart she hoped he would support him, but his present expression gave her no clue at all.

With his nephew out of earshot, he turned to her once more and it seemed incredible to Troy that the voice that had sounded so sternly reprimanding when he spoke to Pietro could change so quickly to the lyrically deep tone that sought her answer. 'Troy? You will come and meet my sister, yes?'

'If you're sure I won't be intruding.'

'I should not have asked you if you were,' he said, and thrusting a hand into a pocket he turned to follow Pietro. 'In a few minutes, Troy!'

That ghostly little 'a' on the end of her name fluttered along her spine as she watched him go, and she hastily took a firmer hold on her parcels and carried them indoors. She had not meant to become involved any more closely with Pietro's family affairs, but somehow it seemed she was not being given the option.

She was tempted to change her dress before she went across to the house, but it was for fear of Lucien's reaction that she refrained. He might think she had tried to make an impression, and she could not face the slightly mocking look she knew would show in those black eyes if he believed it.

Instead she washed her face and hands and put on fresh lipstick, then brushed out her thick reddish hair in front of the mirror, staring critically at her reflection as she did so. She was less apprehensive of meeting Pietro's mother than her travelling companion, and she admitted that the reason was Pietro's unmistakable signs concerning her.

Undoubtedly Signora Arturo would be glamorous and quite possibly beautiful as well; she would undoubtedly be rich, because the Gerolamos and the Gafforis moved in wealthy circles, and even as Troy opened the cottage door she hesitated. Until she came there she had thought herself perfectly self-possessed, but lately she was much less sure of herself and she wished she could do something about it.

Spotting Madame Coron crossing the hall, she called out to her as quietly as she could and still hope to be heard. If she timed her entrance to coincide with the housekeeper's she would feel a little less conspicuous. Madame Coron turned and smiled, waiting until she joined her and quite clearly curious.

'Is something wrong, Mademoiselle Liskard?' she asked. 'How may I assist you?'

Troy inclined her head in the direction of the *salon* where she could hear a babble of animated Italian that did nothing to boost her confidence—suppose Signora Arturo did not speak English! 'I've been invited over to join the party,' she explained, speaking carefully because there were still moments when they did not completely understand one another. 'I wonder if I could come in with you, *madame*. I hate the idea of going in alone with all of them——'

'Ah, *oui, mais oui*!' Obviously her predicament was recognised and appreciated, and Madame Coron led the way to the *salon* door confidently. 'Please to come with me, *mademoiselle*!'

At the door of the *salon* Madame Coron stood back to allow her to step into the room first, then she caught Lucien's eye across the big room and made a sign with her hand that intimated he was wanted. Immediately he came striding across the room, frowning slightly and obviously puzzled, and it was then that Troy realised there had been yet another misunderstanding. Madame Coron had understood her to be in need of a metaphorical hand to hold, but she had summoned Lucien to provide it.

As soon as he was within earshot, the housekeeper explained, with quiet smiles in Troy's direction and shrugs that asked his understanding, until he could be in no doubt that she had shirked coming in alone and had asked for him to lend her moral support. The hand he offered when Madame eventually departed, however, was not merely metaphorical, and Troy flushed when his strong brown fingers squeezed hers tightly and he smiled down at her.

'Are you so nervous, *mia cara*, that you dare not come into the *salon* without Madame Coron to conduct you and beg for my support for you?'

'Oh, it wasn't like that at all,' Troy began, then became aware of more than one interested pair of eyes on them as they came across the big *salon* hand in hand. 'I'm sorry, Lucien,' she murmured while she still had time, and he glanced down at her with black gleaming eyes.

'Why, Troy?' His fingers squeezed hers again, lightly and reassuringly. 'But you need not fear that Bianca will eat you, she is a very gentle soul who spoils all her children, and particularly her firstborn!' He led her by the hand to where a tall smiling woman sat in one of the gilded armchairs—speculating, Troy thought; it showed in her dark eyes, no matter how warm her smile was as Lucien introduced them.

More than ever Troy wished she had changed her dress, for both women were evidently clients of the best designers in Italy. Bianca Gerolamo was beautiful in a dark Latin way that the deep red dress she wore set off perfectly. Shining black hair and wonderful brown eyes, gentle, as her brother said, and friendly too as she proffered her hand.

'This is Signorina Liskard; Troy, Bianca,' he said. 'My sister Bianca; Signora Gerolamo.'

'I am delighted to meet you, *signorina*!' The voice was vaguely reminiscent of Lucien's, with the same velvet overtones but with a slightly more precise English accent, more like her son's. 'I have heard so much about you in such a short time, I think that you must be something very—special, eh?'

Troy laughed, her voice shiveringly unsteady as she tried to think why she should have been mentioned so much in the short time that the visitors had been there. 'I can't imagine in what way, Signora Gerolamo,' she said, and shook her head.

'Pietro has talked of little else but the fact that he was driving with you,' his mother informed her, obviously not averse to the idea. 'And my brother——' She shrugged expressive shoulders and smiled up at Lucien with bright dark eyes. 'I am very pleased to see that you live up to your reputation, *signorina*!'

Troy was in something of a daze when Lucien introduced his other guest, but even so she could not do other than register the contrast in the two women. They had absolutely nothing in common on the surface and if they were such friends it must have been an attraction of opposites. Angela Arturo was shorter than her friend and her hair was a glossy blonde, her figure slim to the point of thinness, and the grey eyes that took in Troy's dress as well as her shape and her slightly flushed face were coldly critical.

Hard fingers briefly touched her hand and were immediately withdrawn, and having conceded that much to courtesy she completely ignored Troy and gave her attention to her host instead. The glossy red mouth smiled, slightly pouted as if in reproach, and Troy wondered if the fact that Lucien seemed to have forgotten that he was still holding her hand had anything to do with it.

'This is a new venture for you, isn't it, Lucien?' she asked in such obviously English English that Troy blinked in surprise. 'I didn't know you took in lodgers!'

Lucien retained his hold on her hand until he saw her seated, then he turned and smiled at Angela Arturo with a gleam in his eyes that suggested malice rather than admiration. 'I have never before been almost run down by a pretty girl in a small car, who thought I was some kind of brigand,' he told her, and turned to wink an eye at Troy. 'Is that right, Troy?'

'I didn't know I nearly ran *you* down as well,' Troy said, and wished her voice sounded less breathless and unsteady. 'I thought it was only the Vincentello children and those wretched goats!'

'It's a pity about the cottage,' Angelo Arturo said smoothly. 'I was rather hoping to steal a few days in your secret nest, Lucien. I'm a bit bored with Rome at the moment, and I know you have your family stay in there from time to time. Not that I mind being in the house, of course,' she added with a sly smile at her host, 'but I was thinking of the propriety of the situation. However——'

Her shrug was pure Italian and Bianca was obviously not quite happy about the way things were going. There was a small frown between her brows as she looked across at her friend.

'You cannot stay here, of course, when I go back, Angela,' she told her, 'but I shall be here for some time, perhaps.' She looked at her son, remarkably silent still, and sighed. 'It depends so much upon Pietro. To stay in the house with me is all right, but not with just Lucien.' Her eyes picked on Troy and she smiled. 'That is why Signorina Liskard has the cottage.'

'And the fact that she has means I *can't* have it,' Angela Arturo complained pointedly. 'I was rather hoping to stay on, Lucien *caro*.'

'Well, you cannot,' Pietro said, speaking up at last. 'Troy's in there and she has a lot to do to her book yet!'

'Pietro!' His mother scolded him gently, but it was clear to Troy that the least Angela Arturo expected of her was for her to move out and make room for her. 'You are writing a book for your grandfather, Lucien tells me,' Bianca went on, skilfully changing the subject. 'I am most interested, *signorina*, you must tell me all about it.'

Troy explained as best she could, and had the interest of at least one of her audience, but the idea of Angela Arturo taking over the cottage had been firmly implanted in her mind, and she found it hard not to dwell on it. Maybe that was why Lucien had invited her over to meet his second guest; with the intention of letting her know, as gently as possible, that the cottage was wanted for someone else. It was a suspicion that grew the more she thought about it, and by the following morning she had promised herself to do something about it.

CHAPTER SEVEN

PIETRO had evidently decided that his mother's presence was going to make very little difference to him. He arrived at the cottage the following morning just before Troy was ready to leave, and she scarcely recognised the fact that she welcomed him with a little less warmth than usual; for one thing because she wanted no more misunderstandings with Lucien about him.

She did let him in, though, and he stood in the middle of the bright little *salon* with his hands in the pockets of his slacks watching her while she gathered her things together. He seldom looked other than immaculate and in the blue slacks and cream shirt he wore this morning, he must have known just how sleek and attractive he looked.

Troy, however, had other matters in mind and took less notice than usual. 'Did you know that Signora Arturo was coming as well yesterday?' she asked, and frowned irritably when he shrugged instead of answering. 'I was caught completely unawares and very embarrassed when Lucien spoke as he did,' she reminded him. 'What's that shrug supposed to convey, Pietro? That you *did* know and you just didn't care that Lucien would automatically assume I'd—connived with you to be out when your mother arrived?'

'It means that I did not intend you to be embarrassed,' Pietro replied with pedantic precision. 'I had not anticipated that Lucien would turn on you as he did, for that I am truly sorry, Troy.' His dark eyes judged her mood and saw it as not outright antagonistic, so he went on. 'It also means that whenever the Signora has the opportunity to get within reach of Lucien she does so, so that

121

it was inevitable that if Mamma told Signora Arturo that she was coming over, then the Signora would find some way of—getting in on the act, eh?'

Troy tested a new ball-point pen by scribbling on the cover of her notebook with it, and asked the question that had been puzzling her ever since she met Angela Arturo the previous evening. 'Is Signora Arturo Italian or English?'

'Both,' said Pietro, tossing off the information carelessly. 'I believe that her *mamma* was English and her *papa* Italian—Mamma said so at one time. Papa does not like her,' he added inconsequentially, and for once Troy was in sympathy with the view of Gerolamo senior; she had not liked Angela Arturo either.

'I thought her English was very—English,' she said by way of explaining her curiosity, and Luigi nodded.

'She learned it from her *mamma*, I expect, for as far as I know she has always lived in Italy. Mamma knew her at school, and she was married to an Italian.'

'Was?' Troy looked up, pouncing on the past tense much more sharply than she realised until she saw Pietro's smile.

He had perched himself on the marble-topped table as he had the first time he visited her, his legs stretched out in front of him and obviously in no hurry to leave. 'They are parted,' he told her, 'though not divorced, of course; but I believe the Signora has plans to take up residence in a country where such things are more easily come by.' He used his hands and rolled his eyes in the same expressive way he had used to convey his meaning last evening when he had heard the identity of Lucien's second guest. Then he laughed. 'Signora Arturo will not give up, you may rest assured!'

Troy slung the big suede bag she often carried on to her shoulder and bent to pick up her sun-glasses, leaving him in no doubt that she was ready to leave. 'In that case,' she said, making up her mind as she spoke, 'it's just as well that I've decided to move out of the cottage and make way for her.'

Obviously the decision took Pietro by surprise and he stared at her for a moment before realising that she was quite serious about it. 'But why?' he asked. 'Why must you go, Troy?'

Troy shrugged, horribly uncertain about her willingness to go, but convinced it was the best thing in the long run. Signora Arturo had been quite pointed in her remarks about the cottage last night. 'Oh, it will make things easier all round if I move on and let things get back to normal,' she said, and Pietro's dark eyes gleamed with laughter as well as a trace of malice.

'You think it is normal for Lucien to have women staying here?' he asked, and laughed as if he found it very amusing. 'You think he brings his *amante* here? You think this really is his secret nest, as Signora Arturo said last night? Oh, Troy, you do not know Lucien very well if you think him so—indiscreet!'

Troy was aware that she was finding the conversation more difficult by the minute, and she shook her head as she moved across nearer the door, pressing home her intention to leave. 'I haven't the slightest idea what constitutes normal around here!' she told him with an edge of sharpness on her voice. 'And I don't think it really concerns me, Pietro. Now, will you please excuse me, I have to get on with some work?'

He got lazily to his feet and his eyes were still smiling, not in the least concerned that he was hindering her, or becoming embarrassing in his frankness. 'You are the first woman he has ever brought here, Troy. Until you came, no one but Gianni and I had stayed in this cottage.' He did not, Troy noticed, say whether the same applied to the house itself, and she had no intention of asking.

'Well, anyway,' she said, as if the matter was cut and dried, 'it will be much more convenient for everyone if I move into an hotel or something——'

'There is no need,' Pietro insisted, but Troy was shaking her head.

'Signora Arturo has to have somewhere, if she does stay on after your mother has gone back to Italy, and she wants the cottage, she said so last night.'

'She does *not* want the cottage,' Pietro argued. 'Can you not see that? It is you that she wishes to see gone, not the cottage available to her.'

His meaning was plain enough and Troy took a firm grip on her bag as she stood in the doorway. 'I'm not going to argue about it,' she stated firmly, 'and I haven't any more time to stand and talk, Pietro. I must get on and try to finish this morning.'

'This morning?' He looked quite startled. 'So soon?'

'The sooner the better now that I've made up my mind,' Troy said, and wished she felt as confidently cheerful as she sounded.

Pietro had that appealingly soulful look on his face again when she looked at him, and she felt rather sorry for him suddenly. He had looked upon her as an ally in his bid for independence and it must seem that she was letting him down at the crucial moment. Not that she had any intention of changing her mind now, but she could not simply walk off and leave him looking as forlorn as he did at the moment.

'I'm writing up my notes,' she told him, and smiled at him as she closed the cottage door behind them. 'Would you get very bored sitting up there with me?'

Normally it was the kind of invitation he would have jumped at, but he glanced at her for a moment in silence and there was something in his eyes that Troy found vaguely discomfiting. His hands still in his pockets, he shrugged without looking at her as they stood in the empty yard.

'I do not think so, thank you, Troy; I have something I must do.' He turned and walked off with a careless wave of his hand and his shoulders hunched. *'Ciao!'*

Troy watched, puzzled by his abrupt departure, until he went in through the back door of the house, then she frowned. There was something in his eyes when he turned briefly before he disappeared that suggested he had something in mind, and she wished she knew what it was.

It was made clear to Troy what Pietro had had in mind when she returned to the cottage later that day. Apparently he had thought it a wise move to forewarn his uncle about her plan before she could surprise him with it, in the hope that he would be more able to persuade her. Lucien came from the house at the same instant she turned into the yard, and the coincidence was such that she suspected he had been watching for her, especially when he obviously wanted to see her.

'Troy!'

He came striding towards her as she opened the cottage door, and she invited him to follow her inside, wishing her self-control was up to letting her appear calm and casual. Putting down her bag on one of the chairs, she turned to face him, the uncertainty she felt showing in the way her eyes just avoided that steady black gaze.

'Is something wrong, Lucien?'

The question was unnecessary, but she asked it just the same and he shook his head with a hint of impatience when she invited him to sit down. Instead he chose to stand in the centre of the *salon* with one hand in a pocket and the other brushing briefly across the back of his head, his fingers running through thick blue-black hair.

'I am hoping that you will reassure me on that point,' he said, and went on without waiting to hear what she had to say. 'I cannot believe what Pietro tells me; that you have decided to leave because my sister has brought Signora Arturo with her, Troy.'

Troy glanced at him briefly, then walked across to the

window on the pretext of rearranging a bunch of honey-suckle that stood in a vase on the sill, busying her fingers while she answered him. 'I wouldn't word it quite like that,' she denied. 'But I noticed that the Signora was disappointed because the cottage was already occupied, and since she is a family friend and you let me have it only as a kindness, it seems right that I should vacate it and make way for her.'

'That is nonsense!'

His vehemence startled her for a moment, and Troy looked at him with uncertain eyes. 'It *is* an obvious solution,' she insisted, 'and I really don't mind, Lucien.'

'It is pointless when you are getting along so well with your work and are so near completing your grand-father's book,' Lucien insisted firmly. 'And your sudden decision is—rash; there is no other word for it, unless it is impulsive! You are impulsive, are you not, Troy?'

It was such a temptation to listen to his reasoning, Troy realised; much more so than when Pietro had tried to persuade her, and she hesitated for a moment, looking up at him curiously. 'But what about Signora Arturo if she wants to stay on?'

Black eyes gleamed at her for a moment, bringing all manner of unbidden thoughts to mind, then he showed his teeth in one of those disturbingly wolfish smiles, and shook his head slowly. 'What about the Signora, Troy?' he asked softly. 'You leave her to me, *mia cara*; you need not concern yourself with what happens to the Signora!'

The smile, the broad wink and his confidence all left her no doubt that she had been very short-sighted about the situation until now, and she despaired of her own slowness. 'Oh no—no, of course not.' She let him know that she had seen the light at last, in a slightly breathless voice, and hastily avoided looking at him.

Of course he did not care whether or not Troy was there, but as long as she was Signora Arturo had no option but to share the house with him if she stayed on after Bianca went back to Italy. Bianca had left her feelings in no doubt, but even she might be swayed by the fact that either Troy had to go or her friend could not take the holiday she had so looked forward to.

Lucien smiled. 'I am glad that you understand, Troy,' he said, and apparently took it that she was convinced of the wisdom of remaining. 'Now I must go, but I will see you later, Troy, eh?' He waved a casual hand as he ducked through the cottage doorway. *'Ciao, cara mia!'*

'Ciao!'

She repeated the now familiar all-purpose word absently while she watched him stride back across the yard, not in the direction of the house this time. Apparently he had some errand in mind concerning the estate, for he disappeared round the end of the house leaving her still gazing after him. Somehow she felt too discomfitingly sure that she was being made use of, and she did not relish the thought at all.

She was rather surprised to find herself banging things about while she made her midday meal, and by the time she had eaten it, she had already reversed her decision yet again. She was not going to stay on simply to suit Lucien Gaffori—if he wanted his lady-friend with him in the house, he could openly say so, and not use the excuse that Troy was occupying the cottage and there was therefore no alternative.

Troy overslept the following morning and it was sheer good fortune that Pietro had not come over to see her; she did not want to see him this morning of all mornings—not yet anyway. She looked around the cottage when she had finished clearing up, and realised how attached to it she had become in the past few weeks. If only things had been different she might have admitted that she could settle quite happily there for good, but not if Lucien was going to bring a succession of mistresses to the house.

The latter thought had grown after a somewhat restless night, and having convinced herself that he was every bit as promiscuous as she had first suspected, she woke with the conviction that Angela Arturo was probably one of many. She had not quite finished her notes yesterday, finding her thoughts too full of other matters to concentrate, but their completion did not depend on her staying in Nemio, she could as easily work elsewhere.

So she told herself as she packed her clothes, but her fingers were horribly unsteady as she coped with the fastenings of her suitcases and she had seldom felt more uncertain in her life. She would pay the rent that was due, and then simply drive off; there need be no fuss and bother, it was quite straightforward.

To save the necessity of returning to the cottage for them, she set her suitcases down just inside the back door while she went in search of Madame Coron. She would be most likely to know where she could find Lucien, and she would like a last word with the housekeeper. Almost inevitably she found her in the big kitchen, and the room smelled deliciously of fresh baked bread and pastries. It was a homely, comfortable picture and once more Troy felt a twinge of regret; she liked Madame Coron and got along well with her.

'Ah, Mademoiselle Liskard!' she said when Troy put her head round the kitchen door. '*Entrez, entrez, s'il vous plaît*—will you please to close the door, *mademoiselle*!'

'Oh yes—I'm sorry, the bread.'

Troy was hesitant; she had not worked out what she was going to say and for the first time she realised that the housekeeper was not going to understand her motives at all. Smiling with forced cheerfulness, she came right into the kitchen watched by Madame Coron while she wiped floury hands on her spotless apron.

'It's all right,' Troy assured her, sensing her anxiety. 'I—I've just decided to leave, that's all. I wondered if you could tell me where I can find Monsieur Gaffori.'

'Leave? You leave, *mademoiselle*? Something is wrong?'

'No, nothing's wrong,' Troy assured her. 'I've simply decided to have a change, that's all, and I'd like to give Monsieur Gaffori my rent—I haven't paid him any so far, but I think this is about right.' She showed her the handful of francs she had, and smiled, struck by a sudden thought. 'Could you give it to him for me, *madame*, do you think?'

'I? *Non, non, mademoiselle!*' Clearly the housekeeper was convinced something was badly amiss, and she refused to even touch the money, but kept her large capable hands folded out of sight under her apron. She looked at Troy with bright narrowed eyes that were frankly curious. 'Does Monsieur know of your departure?' she asked, and Troy shrugged, finding it an increasingly useful mode of communication.

'We talked about it,' she said, 'and I've come to the conclusion I'm right. Please, Madame Coron, can you tell me where I can find him?'

'He is on the drive, *mademoiselle*, with Madame Gerolamo and Madame Arturo. They went in Monsieur's *auto* maybe—an hour or perhaps more. They were not to be long gone.'

Madame Coron was right not to encourage her to simply leave the rent and go, of course, Troy realised it, but she became increasingly convinced that if Lucien tried again to persuade her she would stay on. Realising it, she gave a shaky little laugh and looked once more at the money in her hand.

'I suppose I'd better wait for him,' she said. 'If I might stay here with you, *madame*?'

'*Certainement, mademoiselle*——' She was on the point of asking Troy to sit down when they heard a car outside, and immediately Troy's heart began a wild and completely uncontrollable beat that sounded like the pounding of drums in her ears. *'Voici Monsieur,'* Madame Coron said with certainty. 'Shall I tell him that you wish to speak with him, *mademoiselle?'*

Troy hesitated. It was not going to be easy telling Lucien she had changed her mind a second time, but with his sister and Signora Arturo with him it would be even harder. Even so, it was something she had to do herself, and she shook her head at the housekeeper, at the same time smiling her thanks.

'No, thank you, Madame Coron, I'll see him—I ought to.'

'Très bien, mademoiselle!'

Madame Coron's dark eyes seemed to express approval as well as curiosity, and Troy turned quickly when she heard the front door open and voices in the hall. All three looked vaguely surprised to see her emerge from the kitchen, but Lucien she thought was most sensitive to the fact that something was wrong, although he said nothing but left it to his sister to speak first.

'Buon giorno, signorina!' Bianca's smile did a great deal for Troy's courage but little for her resolution, and she answered absently, her gaze hastening back to Lucien's bold, dark features in search of a clue to his mood.

'Troy?' That barely discernible 'a' lingered musically after her name and sent light shivers through her as she clung tightly to the roll of francs in her hand.

'I wondered if I could have a word with you, Lucien, please.'

There was a note of breathless urgency in her voice and once again it was Bianca who took the initiative, glancing at her brother before putting a hand on Signora Arturo's arm and murmuring something to her in Italian. For a moment it looked as if Angela Arturo would argue the point, but Bianca, like many gentle people, could be very firm, and she pressed her fingers into her friend's arm as she guided her in the direction of the *salon*.

'We will wait for you in the *salon*,' she said to Lucien as they moved away, and a smile included Troy in the invitation. 'You too, Signorina Liskard, perhaps, eh?'

Troy nodded and smiled absently, but she already realised that she would probably never see Bianca Gerolamo again except to say a brief goodbye, perhaps. As soon as they were alone Lucien looked down at her steadily, still without saying anything, although Troy had the feeling that he already knew what was in her mind, and she had never felt more at a loss than she did at the moment.

She heard the *salon* door close behind his visitors and stood clutching the money intended for her rent, wondering why it should be so difficult to tell him she had decided not to stay after all. 'I wanted to give you this and to say goodbye. I don't know if it's right, but I think it is, if it isn't enough——' She gabbled the words out in a breathless little flutter of sound and thrust the money towards him. 'I'm going after all, Lucien, I've decided I'd better. I know you'll understand and also realise how grateful I am for—everything.'

It appalled her to realise how close she was to tears. She had not really visualised saying goodbye to him until this moment, and it was so much harder than she could have anticipated. Lucien looked at the money but made no attempt to take it from her, and she felt more at a loss than ever. A brief upward glance revealed the black eyes on her with that steady, disconcerting look of speculation that could so easily be her undoing.

'I have told you that there is no need for you to go,' he reminded her, almost as if he thought she might have forgotten it. 'We agreed, Troy, did we not?'

'*You* decided,' Troy agreed breathlessly, 'but I've thought it over, Lucien, and I don't—well, I don't think I care to stay any longer in the circumstances.'

'Circumstances?'

His voice sounded genuinely puzzled, and she licked
her dry lips anxiously as she found herself looking for
excuses. 'You said I understood, and I do——'

'Then why will you not stay?'

'No, Lucien, I'd rather go!'

She thrust the money towards him yet again, but still
he refused to even touch it. Instead he narrowed his
black eyes into chips of jet that gleamed between their
thick lashes and made her shiver, then he brushed past
her so roughly that she almost lost her balance, and went
striding across the hall towards the *salon*.

'Lucien——'

'I will not take money from you!' he declared harshly
and without even turning his head. 'You must do as you
please about whether you go or stay!'

The *salon* door closed behind him with an air of
finality, and Troy was left standing alone in the hall and
fighting the need to cry as she had not done since she
was a child. Then the murmur of voices reached her,
speaking in Italian, and she wondered if she had ever in
her life felt more lonely and unhappy.

Madame Coron had been quite anxious about her sudden decision to leave and she had suggested that Troy
wait at least until Pietro returned, but somewhat dazed
by events Troy shook her head. It had occurred to her in
a vague attempt to think constructively that perhaps her
next stop might be the hotel of Maurice Corsi in Benecollocare. He had known her grandfather, however long
ago, and he had been very friendly; he would surely
welcome her as a guest in his hotel.

Having made up her mind, Troy bundled her cases
into the back of her car without waiting for the assistance of the lecherous François, who was never around
when he was needed, then drove off with a deceptively

cheerful wave for Madame Coron who watched from the front doorstep. She tried not to think about what Lucien might at this very moment be saying to Bianca and Angela Arturo about her, but one of them at least would be nothing loath to see her depart, according to Pietro.

It was almost impossible to miss the way to Bene-collocare, for the road was direct and led right through the heart of the forest and down into the valley, towards the sea. The air was fresh and sweet-smelling in the mountains, tingly with the scent of pine where the trees fenced in the road on either side, and there were moments when she had to pull herself up sharply when she remembered how much she had enjoyed the same drive with Lucien a few days ago.

The sun was warm and even in the town itself the air seemed to carry that inescapable scent that flooded over the whole island at this time of year. She would not be very far from the mountains in Benecollocare, but she would also be quite close to the sea and quiet sandy beaches; it was an ideal spot for her.

Turning a corner in the ancient *citadelle* she was once more struck by the sudden contrast between the old and new parts of the town, and before long she recognised Maurice Corsi's small, homely hotel, tucked away in a quiet side street. Leaving the car out front for the moment, she went in through the swing doors, looking around for her host and hoping he was ready with as warm a welcome as he had given Lucien and her.

He did not immediately recognise her, she thought, for he looked a little taken aback, and when he welcomed her it was with much less exuberance and warmth than on that last occasion. Extending a hand, he put on a smile that seemed curiously strained somehow and rather more professional than friendly, almost as if her presence made him uneasy.

'Mademoiselle Liskard—so unexpected!'

'Monsieur Corsi!' She shook hands, but tried in vain

to meet his eyes—he was polite but curiously evasive and there was definitely something odd in his manner, something she could not understand. She recognised nothing this time of the effusive host who had plied her with wine and talked so willingly about his daughter. 'I'd like one of your rooms, please,' she told him. 'My cases are in the car out front, if you could get someone——'

'Alas, *mademoiselle*, I have no room for you!' He cut short her explanation and his thick hands were spread in apology, his shoulders hunched in the classic expression of regret, and Troy stared at him in disbelief.

'Are you telling me that you haven't any rooms vacant?' she asked, unable to believe it. Only a matter of days ago he had admitted to Lucien that he had plenty of vacant rooms, and it simply wasn't feasible that he could have filled them in the time. Puzzled and strangely, uneasy, Troy frowned at him. 'I don't understand that, Monsieur Corsi, you told Lucien only a few days ago that you had rooms——'

'I am sorry, *mademoiselle*!'

He offered no explanation and Troy, from being initially puzzled, was beginning to lose patience. She looked at him and frowned, leaving no doubt that she did not believe him—she could not believe him. 'Surely,' she said, 'you can't have let all the rooms you said were available only days ago—it just isn't possible!'

Troy had been looking for a sympathetic reception in the circumstances, she had had her share of misunderstandings already that morning, and his manner was quite inexplicable. At the same time he seemed so genuinely sorry that she could not help feeling for him, and he must surely have a very good reason for turning her away. Maybe he was having the empty rooms redecorated, although she could not see in that case why he did not say so. In any event he seemed adamant enough not to change his mind and she did not push further—it was his privilege to refuse prospective clients, if he chose.

'Very well,' she said, but relinquished her argument with a sigh that told him plainly enough that she was disappointed in him. 'You know your own business best, Monsieur Corsi, but if you can't put me up, perhaps you can recommend another hotel that can.'

'Another——' He frowned uneasily and it was obvious that the request had taken him off guard. 'There are many visitors to Benecollocare, *mademoiselle*——'

'Not at this time of the year, *monsieur*!' Troy stuck out her chin to let him know exactly how she felt and he was shaking his head, his thick hands clasped close together anxiously. 'Very well,' she said, 'I shall find one for myself! *Au revoir*, Monsieur Corsi!'

'*Mademoiselle!*'

He called after her as she walked rapidly across the foyer, her steps tapping impatiently on the uncarpeted floor, and Troy turned swiftly, hoping it was anger that showed most clearly on her face rather than the hurt she felt as well. He spread his hands while he spoke and they gave the impression of helplessness as well as apology.

'I am sorry I cannot do as you ask, Mademoiselle Liskard. If perhaps you were to return to Nemio for a few days a vacancy would occur; in the meantime——'

'In the meantime,' Troy said, 'I'll find somewhere else, *monsieur*!' She managed at last to hold his gaze and the disappointment she felt showed clearly in her eyes. 'I'm sorry too that you can't find room for me, but I wish I knew why. However——'

She turned once more, but again Monsieur Corsi called her back. His eyes were still evasive and he hesitated to say what he had to say, but eventually shrugged as if he yielded to the inevitable. 'There are two hotels that you might care to try, *mademoiselle*,' he told her, speaking slowly and obviously giving himself time to think. 'There is Le Roi on the Rue Maire and l'Ange which is just around the corner from it on Boulevard du Maire.'

'Thank you, *monsieur*!' She tried to smile but grimaced ruefully when she remembered that she still needed his help. 'Can you give me some idea of how to find them, please? I don't know Benecollocare at all.'

'*Certainement, mademoiselle!*' He used his hands to indicate each turn in the directions he gave her, but spoke too quickly for her to follow easily, and several times she had to stop him and ask him to repeat what he had said. 'It is on the other side of the town from here,' he explained unnecessarily, 'but you will have little difficulty in finding the way, *mademoiselle.*'

'Thank you.' Troy half-turned, then caught his eyes for a moment and frowned curiously, still finding it hard to believe he was deliberately turning her away. 'I wish I knew why you're——' she began, but was interrupted by the shrilling of the telephone in a nearby booth. He had never, she suspected, been so thankful to hear anything in his life as he was that telephone bell, and with a last resigned shrug she turned and went out into the sunlit street again.

It took her ten or fifteen minutes to locate the first of the hotels recommended, and as soon as she drove up in front of it she suspected it was not going to be what she was looking for. For one thing it was far bigger than Maurice Corsi's homely little hotel, and the very grand entrance hall did nothing to encourage her to suppose it would be within her price range. A rather aloof but perfectly polite desk clerk confirmed her suspicion, and she left again feeling rather chastened and very discouraged.

Just around the corner from it, as Maurice Corsi had promised, she found the Boulevard du Maire and the even more grand and expensive l'Ange. In this instance she did not even go inside, but judged the scale of its charges by a brief glimpse into the foyer and a sight of some of its clientele. By the time she returned to her car Troy was feeling not only utterly confused concerning Maurice Corsi's intent, but thoroughly angry too, and it was instinctive, when she drove away from the second of the hotels, to take the direction that led her back to her misleading informant.

She could have found something more suitable by trying some of the smaller hotels, she had no doubt, but first she wanted to get to the bottom of Monsieur Corsi's unco-operative behaviour, and she steered her little car once more down the now almost familiar street. She hated mysteries, and especially when they frustrated and inconvenienced her.

There was no doubt about when she walked into the foyer a second time, but she had barely time to walk across to the reception desk and strike the bell furiously hard before Maurice Corsi appeared. In this instance she noticed quite definitely the uneasy glance he gave over his shoulder, and a small but growing suspicion lurked in the bright anger in her blue eyes as she faced him.

'Monsieur Corsi,' she began, breathlessly hasty in her anxiety to let him know how she felt, 'I'd like to know *why* you sent me on a wild-goose chase all across Benecollocare when you must have known perfectly well that both the places you recommended were well beyond my means! I don't know why you refused to let me have a room here or why you sent me off on a fool's errand to the other end of town, but I mean to!' Troy seldom lost her temper, but when she did it was an explosion of temperament that her French grandfather had recognised as an extension of his own Gallic emotionalism. 'You must have a reason, Monsieur Corsi, though for the moment I can't imagine what it is. I only know that I'm so furious I could hit someone!'

Maurice Corsi stood watching her and she suddenly realised with a stab of surprise that he was smiling. 'I was—requested to mislead you, *ma chère mademoiselle*, that is my reason,' he said, and Troy stared at him, wondering if he had suddenly taken leave of his senses. 'It was for a good reason, I am assured,' he went on, seeing her momentarily dumbstruck. 'To delay you, merely.'

Troy drew a breath, about to demand further explanation, when something just within the scope of her vision caught her eye and she turned her head swiftly. 'If you wish to hit someone, Troy,' Lucien told her coolly, 'I suggest it is me and not poor Maurice, who did only as I asked him.'

'You?'

Dazedly Troy stared across at the dark, brigand's face with its gleaming black eyes and wished she felt less elated at seeing him there. The last time she had seen Lucien he had been leaving her to go and join his guests in the *salon*, disclaiming any interest in what she did from then on. Now he was looking across at her with an expression in his eyes that suggested he was not only vaguely amused by her threat of violence, but might even be glad to see her again.

Flicking a nervous tongue over dry lips, Troy shook her head. 'What are you doing here, Lucien?'

'Visiting an old friend.'

She did not notice for the moment that Maurice Corsi was now quite relaxed and restored to his former smiling self, even though he flicked a wary eye between the two of them. Then Lucien left the doorway of the living quarters and came across the foyer in long easy strides, something in his manner speeding up her heartbeat until she felt as if she was spinning round and round where she stood.

'Also I came to take you back with me,' he added as matter-of-factly as if he was reclaiming something that belonged to him, and Troy stepped back instinctively when he came close enough to touch.

'We went through all this before I left,' she reminded him, anxiously keeping her distance.

'And will again,' Lucien promised with a hint of a smile as he put a hand on her arm. 'But this is not the place to discuss such matters, Troy. Come!'

'Where to?' She asked the question breathlessly, and he laughed, an almost soundless expression of amusement that brought a swift flush to her cheeks.

'To Maurice's *salon, mia cara*, where it is less public, eh?'

It was a practical enough suggestion if they were to discuss the pros and cons of the situation, although she did not quite see what good further discussion could do, but she hesitated only briefly, then allowed the hand on her arm to persuade her into the privacy of their host's inner sanctum.

Lucien suggested she sit down, but to Troy any form of relaxation was out of the question at the moment and she chose to remain on her feet. Looking up at him, she avoided direct contact with those disturbing eyes, but tried to make it look as if she did not mind facing him.

'I don't know why you came all this way simply to start the whole thing again,' she told him, then frowned suspiciously when something else occurred to her. 'How did you know I was here, Lucien?'

He was smiling and not in the least deterred by her discouraging response, she realised. 'Madame Coron informed me,' he told her, 'and I telephoned to Maurice.'

'Lucien, you had no right!'

Nevertheless the idea of him coming to find her aroused all sorts of infinitely disturbing thoughts which she did her best to quell before they got out of hand, and she had a strangely lightheaded feeling as she stood facing him in the cool of the little *salon*. She was no longer sure whether or not Maurice Corsi was still with them, but she thought not.

'It doesn't alter anything,' she said in a small tight voice that she sought hard to steady.

'You will not come back, Troy?' The lingering echo after her name brought a tingle to her nerve ends and Troy tried to repress the responsive shiver. Shaking her head as much to deny her own reflexes as to answer his question, she saw the way he raised one black brow. 'You are being stubborn, are you not?'

He passed the opinion coolly and as if it was an un-arguable fact so that she flushed warmly and gave him a brief reproachful look. 'I don't quite see why you're being so insistent about my coming back,' she said. 'Why does it matter so much, Lucien? You don't need the rent or you'd have taken it when I offered it.'

Lucien pushed one hand into a pocket and seemed to be considering the question. His black eyes were half hidden by lowered lids and gave his rugged face a staggeringly sensual look that stirred her senses to an urgent response, so that she looked down at her hands rather than at him after one brief glance.

'You were my first paying guest,' he reminded her after a moment or two. 'You have given me ideas—about taking in guests, of course,' he added, but smiled in such a way there was no mistaking his meaning. 'Being a land*lord* is a new experience for me, Troy, and I am quite enjoying it!'

'But——' Troy used her hands in a tell-tale gesture of helplessness; he must know she was on the point of yielding. 'The situation hasn't changed with Signora——'

'Have I not told you to leave the matter of the Signora to me?' he demanded, then laughed softly at the expression on her face. 'And you have no need to look so, *cara mia*! For the time being Bianca has decided to stay with Pietro, so you need have no fear for anyone's virtue!'

Troy would have protested, she opened her mouth to do so, but it was no more than a breath of sound that died on her lips when he bent his head suddenly and quite unexpectedly and pressed his lips to hers, lingering for a moment while she coped with a spinning chaos of emotions. It was no more than a light caress, but it was effective enough to make resistance impossible, and when he spoke that deep lyrical voice added its persuasion too.

'So, you come back, eh?' He kissed her again in the same light, caressing manner, then laughed again as he looked down into her face, taking her consent for granted. 'And now we all eat, yes?'

Dazedly it occurred to Troy that she liked the idea and she nodded. 'I am hungry,' she told him in a small and slightly husky voice.

'*Bene!*' Lucien said softly and with obvious satisfaction. 'Then we shall eat!'

CHAPTER EIGHT

MAURICE CORSI had given them an excellent lunch and Troy was feeling more relaxed than she had for some time as she walked with Lucien along the Quai des Rameaux. The quay ran for most of the way along Benecollocare's waterfront and made a pleasant walk, being wide and paved and shaded by palms that gave it a touch of glamour. Further on, past the pier where the boats came in, there was a sandy beach with excellent bathing, but nothing was further from Troy's mind at the moment than bathing.

She had thought to cut herself off from all contact with Lucien and his family when she made her determined exit earlier that morning, but she could see now the inevitability of her involvement. It had begun, she realised, the moment she opened her eyes on that narrow mountain road and saw Lucien standing beside her car; it had deepened when she had found Pietro in her cottage and then allowed him to tell her his reason for being there.

Maurice Corsi had joined them for lunch, thoroughly open now about his deception and enjoying the joke enormously, but his presence had rather restricted their conversation to more general matters. It had been Lucien's suggestion that he should show her the waterfront while they were there, and Troy had accepted eagerly because she made no attempt to deny it to herself that she enjoyed being with him. Even though there were matters he could raise at any moment that she would find more than discomfiting.

The harbour was wide and sweeping, the water placid and smooth as silk and a kind of grey-blue in colour,

with small boats in bright, bold colours bobbing at
anchor and lining the sea walls. It was backed by rows
of tall buildings with dark slate roofs and layer upon
layer of floors as all Corsican buildings seemed to be,
neat rectangular windows ranged across their faces like
rows of narrowed eyes. Sturdy as fortresses and with
thick strong doors fostering the illusion, even where the
palm trees fluttered their patterns over stone walls.

'It's beautiful!' Troy passed the opinion after a fairly
long silence and looked at Lucien as she did so, smiling.

'I am glad you like it.'

'Don't you?' She challenged his opinion and he smiled
only faintly as he answered.

'I love Corsica,' he said. 'It is all beautiful to me.'

Another silence followed. Not a flat uneasy silence
lacking in sympathy, but one that denoted two people
seeking ways of beginning a conversation that could in a
matter of seconds change the tone of their present com-
panionship to something less comfortable, and both hesitant about taking the first step. Eventually it was Troy
who did so, simply because she felt herself becoming
much too affected by the physical presence of her companion; far too conscious of him as a man.

It was so easy to imagine that they were lovers, strolling along the sunlit waterfront together, their faces
dappled by the shadowing palms and their bodies
warmed by the spring sunshine. Such a growing awareness of him affected her senses and made her anxious to
bring matters back to a more practical level and, looking
out across the water, she stopped for a moment to watch
a small cargo boat leaving the pier at the far end of the
harbour.

Picking on a safer subject than her own recent ab-
scondence, she chose a subject most certainly more close
to his heart. 'What's going to happen about Pietro,
Lucien?' she asked.

He stood close beside her so that she was no less

aware of him than before, his eyes narrowed against the bright sun on the water, and from the ready way he answered it was fairly evident the same subject had been already on his mind. 'Bianca is planning to remain for a while in the hope that Pietro will return to Italy with her.'

'Do you think he will?'

Lucien shrugged, though it was nothing like as careless a gesture as it appeared, she knew. 'I do not know,' he confessed frankly. 'But in the meantime he will be spending more time in the vineyards with me in the hope of learning something about growing grapes. I think,' he added with a faint smile, 'that he might be surprised to discover he has to work!'

'And you think that will be enough to discourage him?'

'Do you not?' Lucien countered swiftly, then shook his head before she could voice an opinion. 'As it happens, Troy, you are to be the one who decides whether or not he returns to Rome or continues with his little rebellion!'

A swift sideways glance noted her startled reaction and Troy stared at him, momentarily stunned. 'Me?'

From his expression it would seem that whatever he had to say, the words were not easily come by and he was frowning slightly. 'So Pietro has decided,' he told her.

Noting the frown and remembering how she had been accused of encouraging Pietro, she shook her head firmly. 'I don't know what you're trying to say, Lucien, but nothing Pietro does is any of my business, you've said so yourself on more than one occasion, and I agree with you! I can't get involved—I don't *want* to be involved in purely family affairs!'

'I am afraid that you are already involved, *cara mia,* quite inextricably,' he said quietly and with such firmness that Troy frowned at him.

'I don't see how,' she argued. 'I haven't offered advice

or even expressed an opinion, not since that first time you overheard me and accused me of encouraging him. If Pietro has—done anything, then he's done it on his own and without any influence from me!'

Lucien said nothing for a moment, but a light finger-tip touch on her arm persuaded her to continue their stroll along the quay. He moved more closely beside her when they resumed walking and the hand lingered, the finger-tips just brushing her skin and sending a tingling shiver of sensation along her arm. She did not remember ever having been quite so physically aware of him before and it was doubly disturbing because she suspected he meant her to feel as she did.

'You have—what is it you say?—got under his skin,' he told her, and Troy glanced up at him warily. 'It is natural enough,' he went on coolly, 'you are a very lovely girl and Pietro is at a very impressionable age!'

'Lucien, I don't——'

'However, it was rather unexpected,' he went on, ignoring her attempt to interrupt, 'when he told us that he intends to be guided by your judgment. He has decided to ask your opinion and to abide by whatever answer you give him. You are to be an unbiased judge, *cara mia*, someone outside the family; and whatever you say he will do, he has promised.'

'Lucien, I can't!'

An unbiassed judge! Pietro's true supposition was exactly the opposite, for he already knew her opinion; she had let him know it quite innocently, shortly after he told her his reason for leaving home, and Lucien had overheard it too. If Pietro was leaving the final judgment to her it was in the confident belief that she would decide his way.

She came to a halt in the shade of one of the palm trees and its fluttering shadow added sapphire darkness to her blue eyes when she looked up at him. 'Don't you see,' she went on when he did not reply, 'I can't take the responsibility of deciding anything as important as that? Pietro already knows that I think he should be allowed to choose his own career, I'd think the same way who-ever it was! He'll be sure I'd speak in his favour!'

'Then do so, Troy, please!'

Troy stared up at him, at the dark strong features that so seldom showed the full depth of his feelings, and she shook her head. A wooden seat stood on the quay, half in and half out of the sun, and facing across the water, and Lucien led her to it. Sitting down beside her with one elbow resting on the back, he clasped his long brown hands loosely together and studied them closely while she watched his face. Then realisation dawned at last and she shook her head slowly.

'You really want me to!' she breathed, still watching his face. 'You want me to tell Pietro to dig his heels in, don't you, Lucien?'

He neither confirmed nor denied it for a moment, but he glanced up and a brief sardonic smile hovered fleet-ingly about his mouth, then he shrugged. 'How can I pass an opinion, Troy? I am not unbiassed, I cannot be in my position, you can see that, and already I am considered a bad influence——'

'You mean letting them have the cottage when they're here?' she asked, slightly breathless when she remem-bered the implications that had accompanied the in-formation, and Lucien eyed her enquiringly. 'I heard it from you *and* Pietro,' she told him hastily. 'He seemed to think you were very understanding.'

'I am flattered!'

'But it wasn't the kind of recommendation that would go down very well with someone who was—well, as strict as Pietro's father sounds. I can see that he would consider you a bad influence.'

Black eyes regarded her steadily for a moment and to Troy it seemed that both amusement and resentment lurked somewhere in their implacable depths. 'From your observations, I conclude that it is an opinion you share,' he said, and Troy shook her head hastily.

'Not at all,' she denied, 'Pietro could do a lot worse than follow your example—as far as his career is concerned especially. Your brother-in-law can hardly fault you there, surely.'

'On the contrary,' he said with a smile, 'my moral character does not concern him nearly as much as the fact that I have chosen to be a wine-grower like my father.' He put his arm along the back of the seat behind her and laughed shortly as he went on to explain. 'My father was a shepherd, *mia cara*,' he reminded her dryly, 'and Pietro senior wishes that both his wife's parents were equally well born. Bianca has the patrician good looks of our mother's family, the elegance and the social graces——' An eloquent shrug dismissed such virtues as part of his own make-up, though it was doubtful if it was with any sort of regret. 'I am very much my father's son!'

'And have every reason to be proud of the fact, from what I've heard of him!' Troy declared, and a long forefinger traced a light caressing line along her upper arm by way of appreciation.

There was obviously social prejudice involved and to Troy it seemed a rather outmoded situation, though she refrained from saying so at the moment. Lucien went on, talking quietly and apparently accepting his brother-in-law's attitude, although she felt that more passionate feelings must lurk somewhere below that cool exterior. Lucien was, after all, very Corsican and any kind of slight would arouse a brooding sense of resentment in someone whose forebears had indulged in the bloody revenge of the vendetta.

'There is no fault to find with Mamma, of course,' he went on. 'She is of what Pietro senior would term good stock—blue blood, eh? To grow grapes as the Illaris did, to merely lend a great name to the produce, is not the same as sweating in the fields as my father did when he went first to Italy. Mamma is acceptable, but Papa——' He shook his head and shuddered with affected distaste, but there was no real amusement in the smile that slashed his brown face for only a moment. 'A Corsican shepherd is not the kind of father-in-law that a man like Pietro Gerolamo likes to admit to, no matter how much he adores Bianca; and for Pietro to wish to learn as his grandfather did, as I did, from the very bottom upward, is not to be encouraged!'

'A thorough snob!' Troy decreed, heedless of whether or not she was being tactful, and Lucien put back his head and gave a great shout of laughter.

'*Sì, piccola,*' he applauded, 'a thorough snob, as you say! Oh, Troy, my so excellent brother-in-law would not approve of you either!' He was shaking his head, taking note of the faint flush in her cheeks, his black eyes gleaming. 'You know the tradition of service in the Gerolamo family?' he asked, returning to their original conversation, and Troy nodded. 'Then you know what is expected of Pietro.'

'He told me,' she said, and folded her hands together while she too rested one elbow on the back of the seat they shared. 'I thought from your behaviour until now that it was what you expected of him too, Lucien. Now I'm not at all sure what you feel about it.'

His eyes were deep and unfathomable as he studied her for a moment, then he shook his head slowly. 'I happen to believe that it is easier to be happy growing grapes than sitting in an Embassy office,' he told her, 'but that is something I cannot say either to Pietro or to my sister, who is above all a loving and obedient wife. You can say so, *mia cara,* because you have nothing to lose in this matter, so I am asking you to settle it for us.'

It was a no less nerve-racking request the second time around, and Troy reflected for a moment. 'For whose sake should I be settling it, Lucien? Yours or Pietro's?'

It was so difficult to know what he was thinking when she could not see his eyes for thick black lashes, and he got to his feet before he gave her an answer to her question, reaching down to take her hand and pull her up beside him. 'For Pietro's,' he said with a faint smile. 'Or for mine, *mia cara*—you may choose.'

It was very much like returning home when she came back to the cottage, Troy found, but it surprised her to realise that Pietro did not even know she had gone until he saw her return with Lucien. He came across to the cottage almost before she was inside, frankly curious about her reasons both for going away and then for allowing herself to be brought back. From the doorway of her bedroom he watched while she unpacked her things again and put them away, his dark eyes quizzical. 'How did Lucien persuade you to come back?' he asked, after she gave him her reason for going, then he laughed and winked an eye. 'Or shouldn't I ask?'

Troy continued putting one of her dresses on to a hanger and answered without looking round at him. 'You can ask anything you like, Pietro! There's nothing secret about why I came back, any more than why I went. I thought I ought to go, and Lucien made it clear that I need not, that's all there is to it!'

'Just like that?' Clearly he suspected a much more complicated situation, but he was primarily interested in his own situation at the moment, and he was more serious suddenly as he came on into the room and leaned both arms on the bottom rail of the old-fashioned bed. 'Did he tell you of my plan, Troy?'

Troy carried on with what she was doing while she answered him; it was easier that way. 'Yes, he told me, Pietro, though I don't like it.'

Apparently her tone surprised him and he watched

her with his dark eyes narrowed suspiciously for a moment. 'I suppose he tried to talk you out of it?' he guessed, and Troy turned around and looked at him.

'No,' she said, 'he didn't. As a matter of fact——' She stopped when it dawned that the last thing Lucien wanted was for his nephew to realise he had his support. Pietro was impulsive enough to tell his father so. 'He left it entirely to me,' she said, folding carefully and apparently completely absorbed in what she was doing.

'And?'

There was a hint of arrogance in the question that reminded her so much of Lucien that she almost smiled. More probably it was attributable to his father's influence, but it was unlikely that Pietro Gerolamo senior was possessed of any more pride and arrogance than the brother-in-law he despised, no matter what his pedigree.

It was curious how she suddenly felt so much older than he did, and she wondered if Pietro wasn't still quite a schoolboy even though he was nearly eighteen years old. 'If I have to decide for you, Pietro,' she told him, 'I can't do it on the spur of the moment.'

'Troy!' It was not the reaction he expected, and Troy felt rather mean for keeping him in suspense, but she still could not bring herself to take that irrevocable step. She still shied away from becoming too closely involved in the inevitable family conflict. Pietro was angry, it showed in his dark eyes, but she could not help that. 'Troy, you are not going to let me down!'

'I'm simply taking time to think before I act,' she reasoned. 'I have to be sure, Pietro, and I don't intend to be—hustled! Now will you please let me get on with something, or I shall be sorry I came back.'

Both malice and laughter showed in his eyes as he thrust both hands into the front pockets of the tight blue jeans he wore, and he turned and swaggered confidently across to the door. 'When Lucien has been to the trouble of bringing you back here?' he said, and turned to wink an eye. 'Oh, I don't think that's likely, is it, Troy?'

Troy had another visitor the following morning. A rather unexpected one but none the less welcome, for she had already decided that she liked Bianca Gerolamo. It was not Bianca's fault if her husband was so hidebound by tradition that he gave it priority even over his son's happiness.

'Please come in, *signora*,' she said, opening the door wide, and Bianca nodded her thanks, bringing the heady scent of musk into the little *salon* with her. 'Won't you sit down?'

Troy's liking for Bianca had been almost instant, but she took time now to notice features about his sister that Lucien had pointed out when he spoke of her. Her features were cast in the clean-cut patrician mould; fine and aristocratic in contrast to Lucien's rugged and earthy strength. She had style and elegance too, but no hard edge to her elegance as Angela Arturo did; Bianca was gentle and charming and she probably doted on her handsome elder son, just as Lucien claimed.

Troy was pleased to see her, but the less happy about the prospect of discussing Pietro's wild scheme for deciding whether or not he was to go on defying his father dismayed her." She had absolutely no doubt that that was in Bianca's mind, and she only wished it need not be so.

'I am not disturbing your work?' Bianca looked around as if she expected to see more obvious signs of industry. Seeing none, she looked across at Troy curiously as she seated herself in one of the armchairs and crossed her slim legs elegantly. 'You have almost completed your book, so Pietro tells me.'

'Very nearly,' Troy agreed. 'I still have the whole thing to type out, of course, but that can easily be done when I get back to England.'

'Which will not be yet, I hope,' Bianca said, and Troy

was convinced there was more than just politeness behind the wish.

'Not just yet, *signora*.' She laughed a little self-consciously as she added, 'Although I could quite easily complete my notes without staying on in Nemio.'

For a moment Bianca's eyes twinkled with the same kind of mischief that showed in her son's so often, and she smiled. 'Ah, but my brother thinks that you should complete them here, yes?' She was almost immediately serious again, although she settled her gaze on her own elegantly swinging foot while she spoke rather than look at Troy. 'It is most unlike Lucien to insist so firmly that you return, Signorina Liskard,' she told her. 'I do not know if you realise that. I have never before known him to—pursue a woman quite so determinedly.'

'Hardly that, *signora*!' It was a matter that Troy preferred not to discuss, especially with someone whom she suspected was rather more discerning than first impressions suggested, but she smiled vaguely and shook her head. 'Leaving the cottage was an impulsive gesture on my part; I was thinking it would make things easier for Signora Arturo.'

'Ah!' Apparently she had confirmed a suspicion. 'That was very thoughtful of you, *signorina*, but quite unnecessary; when I return to Rome, Signora Arturo will be returning with me. There is no question about it,' she added with that hint of firmness that Troy had noticed once before. 'My brother knows that.'

It was not easy to imagine this kind, gentle woman laying down the law to a man like Lucien, and yet Troy felt bound to believe that Bianca had done just that. Maybe it had been Bianca who sent him to fetch Troy back too. The thought only now occurred to her and it was a discomfiting one.

'Was it your idea that Lucien came after me, *signora*?' she asked, impulsive as always, and Bianca looked faintly shocked.

'Oh, but certainly not, Signorina Liskard! Lucien realised his mistake almost immediately, but alas too late to prevent you from leaving. He lost no time once he had discovered from Madame Coron where it was you intended to go.'

'I see.'

Troy wished there was something she could do about the slight warmth in her cheeks, for Bianca undoubtedly noticed it. Being the woman she was, however, she smoothly changed the subject, though the alternative was one that was only slightly less discomfiting to Troy.

'But it is concerning Pietro that I wished to speak with you, *signorina*—may I call you Troy as Lucien and Pietro do?'

'Oh, but of course, please do!' The gesture of friendship was more pleasing than the prospect of discussing Pietro, but it was inevitable, Troy supposed, and she accepted it with a smile of resignation.

Bianca studied her own slender fingers for a moment and while she did so Troy tried to guess what her feelings were regarding her son. Bianca Gerolamo, she suspected, was exactly what Lucien had called her—a loving and obedient wife, but it was by no means certain that she shared her husband's sense of tradition regarding Pietro's future. It was just possible that no one had so far informed Pietro's father that his son's decision whether or not to obey him depended upon the word of a stranger, and Troy felt her position keenly. More so now that she was face to face with Bianca on the question.

'Lucien has told you of Pietro's plan?' Bianca asked. 'That he wishes to become a wine-grower?'

Troy nodded. 'I also know your husband's wishes,' she said, 'but so far I haven't heard your opinion, Signora Gerolamo.'

'Bianca, please.' Her dark eyes hovered uncertainly, not quite meeting hers, and Troy could gather nothing of her inner feelings yet. 'I wish only for my son to be happy, Troy,' she said after a moment.

'And you think he'll be happy being a diplomat?'

Bianca was uneasy. It must be very uncomfortable for her, Troy realised, caught between a strong-willed, autocratic husband and an equally strong-minded son, and she felt sorry for her. 'It is what my husband wishes for him,' she said. Then she used her hands in the same expressive, gesturing pleas that Pietro so often employed, seeking not so much her approval as her understanding. 'It is not easy to explain, Troy. My husband is a good man and he loves Pietro dearly, but he is—how is it?—bound up in tradition and determined to see Pietro follow him into a career that his family have followed for generations.'

'But you have two sons,' Troy pointed out, wondering if she was being quite fair to shift the interest to a younger brother.

But Bianca's troubled face softened into a smile when she considered her younger son. 'Ah, *caro* Gianni,' she said. 'If only he had arrived first and was the one christened Pietro like his father, there would be no problem!'

'Oh, I see.'

It had to be Pietro, Troy saw it more clearly now, because he was the one who carried the label of the eldest son, the one who was expected to carry the tradition of the Gerolamos into the next generation. What no one yet seemed to have taken into account was the fact that Gaffori blood also flowed in Pietro's veins. It was the tradition of living and working close to the land that he had inherited from the strong-minded, courageous old man who was Lucien's father that he wished to follow, not the more exalted steps of his father's family.

'Pietro is too much of a Gaffori, isn't that right, Bianca?' she asked, and she knew from Bianca's expression that she was right.

'You know about my father coming from Nemio, of

course,' she said, never for a minute doubting her knowledge. 'It is a very close tie the Corsicans have with their island, Troy, and it is very hard to break, even for a third generation, like Pietro. Lucien felt the pull and he came here, put down his roots here, now Pietro wishes to follow suit, and it is much more difficult for his father to understand.'

'It's a perfectly natural thing to want,' Troy said, and Bianca nodded slowly.

'Pietro is as much Gaffori as Gerolamo.'

She did not smile, but it seemed to Troy that there was the same air of satisfaction about her that she had noticed in Lucien sometimes. They both seemed to have the ability to convey how they felt without committing themselves verbally, and Troy guessed that if she advised Pietro to stand his ground he would do so with the support of his mother as well as his uncle, although neither of them would have made a single gesture of defiance themselves.

'I am so glad that you understand how Pietro feels,' Bianca told her, and caught her eye for a moment. 'He has agreed to accept your decision, Troy, and I wished for you to know how deeply he feels. You are impartial, you cannot be accused of being biassed in favour of either side.'

'So Lucien pointed out,' Troy said. 'But it doesn't mean I have to like being the pivot of something as controversial as this, Bianca.'

It would involve a family upheaval whichever way she chose, Troy guessed, but perhaps rather less than if Lucien and Bianca brought their true feelings into the open. Pietro would not give in gracefully if she went against him, whether or not he had agreed to abide by her decision; and the very least she could expect was a very unpleasant scene with Pietro senior if she cast in favour of continuing disobedience. Probably it would satisfy that Corsican taste for drama that Pietro had mentioned once, but Troy had no desire to become part of a controversy involving both Corsican and Italian temperaments. Her only hope was that Pietro might relieve her of the responsibility.

'I shall try and get out of it if I possibly can, Bianca,' she told her, but Bianca's dark eyes offered little hope as she got up from her chair.

'I do not think that is possible, Troy,' she said. 'I know my son.'

'And I,' Troy told her with a wry smile, 'am beginning to wish I didn't!'

Troy could as easily have done what she was doing in the comfort of the cottage, in fact it would have been much simpler to write on the surface of a table instead of resting her book on her knees, but then she would not have been able to enjoy the pleasure of the mountain-side. The sun was quite hot for spring, but tempered by the mildly humid *mistral*, and as ever the temptation to laze was almost irresistible.

With her notebook rapidly filling she scribbled industriously for a while, refusing to let her surroundings creep in on her concentration and distract her, and then, as she glanced up briefly, she caught sight of Pietro climbing the slope towards her and sighed resignedly. He was undeniably good company, but there was little chance of getting much done while he was with her.

'Why do you not wait for me?' he demanded, only slightly out of breath as he dropped down beside her. 'Are you avoiding me, Troy?'

She made a deliberate show of carrying on with what she was doing and shook her head, looking up only when she had completed the page. 'Not exactly,' she denied, 'although I was hoping to have the chance of finishing this today.'

'So that you go back to England?' she asked. 'What is your hurry, Troy? You like it here and there is no worry about the cottage, Lucien has made that quite clear to you. So why the hurry to finish?'

Troy sketched a small and quite good drawing of a cyclamen on the top of the page, then regarded it critically for a second before she answered. 'The flowers are going over now,' she observed. 'I came at the best time—in spring.'

'Nonsense!' Pietro declared shortly. 'There are always flowers on Corsica!' He placed a hand over hers and stilled the pen for a moment while he looked into her face. 'What about me, Troy? You cannot go until you have said what I should do.'

It was a matter that she had been hoping to avoid, but there had been little hope of it in the circumstances she had to allow. Pushing away his hand, she added curling leaves to the cyclamen, then shaded them in, still without looking up. 'I'd like to know just how serious you are about that, Pietro,' she said, and sensed his sudden frown when he turned to look at her. 'I mean,' she went on before he could say anything, 'I sometimes wonder if you're simply trying your wings by defying your father, or if you really want to follow in the footsteps of Lucien and your Nonno Gaffori.'

'You think I am not serious?'

She might have insulted him, from the tone of his voice, but Lucien had said he was to accompany him this morning, and instead Pietro had come in search of her. It did not suggest a very serious application to the study of viniculture, and she wondered if he was already changing his mind. Whether Lucien had been right to suggest he might be put off by the amount of work involved.

Looking up, she caught his eye. 'Weren't you supposed to go with Lucien this morning?' she asked, and he gave her such a sly smile that she found it distinctly suspicious for some reason she could not define.

'I was supposed to go,' he agreed, 'and I would have

gone willingly, but Lucien has driven with Signora Arturo to Benecollocare for shopping.'

'Oh, I see.'

Troy was surprised at her own reaction, though she did her best to appear unaffected because Pietro was watching her from the corner of his eyes and they gleamed brightly with speculation. 'Of course they will have lunch,' he guessed, apparently musing aloud, 'and then take a stroll, perhaps; you know yourself how Lucien is. So, my education for today must be the study of wild flowers, not of vines, eh?'

'I hardly think so,' Troy told him, unwittingly short, 'I have to finish these notes and I haven't time to lecture you on wild life!'

'Do you suppose Lucien is lecturing the Signora on wild life?' Pietro suggested, then laughed aloud and rolled back to gaze up at the sky with his long length stretched out beside her. 'My uncle is what you call in England a dark horse, eh, Troy?' Dark eyes speculated on her reaction from below lazily drooped lids, and he was still smiling. 'He shows a face like a stern moralist, but——'

'I haven't the slightest desire to sit here and listen to a run-down on Lucien's morals!' Troy told him sharply, and from the way she was gathering together her bag and her notebooks it was clear that she was going to move away.

'Oh, Troy!' He sat up, reaching for her hand and keeping her sitting while he looked into her face with such appeal that she could not hope to keep up her ill humour for very long. 'I am sorry,' he said, and indeed looked so contrite she had to believe him. 'You will forgive me, yes?'

'I'll forgive you,' Troy promised after a moment's thought, 'as long as you promise not to mention Lucien again.'

'I just——'

'Not one word!' Troy insisted, and he looked at her for a moment then produced one of his swift, boyish grins and lay back once more, his weight crushing the prickly softness of wild thyme and filling the air with its scent.

'Not one word,' he vowed, then laughed suddenly and apparently without reason so that she looked at him sharply for a moment.

He was quiet for long enough for her to get on with transcribing her rough notes into the exercise book she was to type from when she eventually reached that stage. Stretched out beside her, he was apparently quite happy to let her work for the moment and he seemed to be half asleep until he sat up suddenly and reached into a pocket for a packet of cigarettes. Troy had never seen him smoke before and she looked at him curiously, noting that he was smoking the same long dark cigarettes that Lucien smoked.

'I didn't know you were a smoker, Pietro,' she said, and he shrugged with what she felt sure was assumed carelessness.

'Sometimes I do.' He expelled smoke from between pursed lips, just as she had seen Lucien do so often, so that the idea that he was copying his uncle was irresistible. Looking at her through the resultant haze, he smiled enquiringly. 'You don't mind, Troy?'

'Not in the least,' she denied, but glanced at the sun-dried maquis that surrounded them and shook her head. 'I wouldn't have thought it was a good idea to smoke out here, though, not when everything is so dry—it's ages since we had rain.'

'You think I am foolish enough to start a fire?'

She should have known he would resent being criticised for it, however mildly, for he was very sensitive to criticism that cast doubts on the fact that he was anything but a grown man. He was incredibly touchy about the fact that he was still in that limbo between boyhood and manhood and resented any reminder that he was, or should be, still at school. In the event Troy said no more, but she still kept a wary eye on the hand that held the cigarette, while she continued to write.

She was getting on quite well, all things considered, when she heard Pietro give a soft whistle of surprise and looked around at him curiously. He was pointing downhill in the direction of the road, and as she followed his direction a car turned on to the track leading to the house. A familiar black car with two people in it.

'No lunch, it seems,' Pietro said, and laughed.

Troy's heart was banging away hard at her ribs while she watched the car's progress and tried to convince herself that the sense of satisfaction she experienced was quite uncalled for. The car bounced and bumped along the familiar track and she could almost imagine Signora Arturo's mood at the moment. She wanted to smile and eventually she found the need irresistible as she bent over her notebook once more.

'I wonder why,' she said, and Pietro's chuckle brought her head up once more.

Catching his eye the impulse to laugh was impossible to resist, and Pietro made it worse by joining in until their laughter soared into the warm spring air and lingered in faint echoes among the hills. His dark eyes gleamed with malice as well as the warmth of laughter as they watched his uncle's car disappear behind the buildings.

'I think perhaps the Signora is very disappointed,' he observed, and obviously relished the fact. 'For me, I am relieved to know that I shall not be acquiring *cara* Angela for my aunt!'

Troy turned swiftly and looked at him, her eyes startled for the moment and forgetting that Pietro had already told her how determined Angela Arturo was where Lucien was concerned. 'Was there ever any chance of her becoming your aunt?' she asked, and he shrugged.

'Maybe not,' he conceded. 'But the fact that she has not been given lunch is very reassuring!' He held her gaze with steady dark eyes, mischief lurking in their depths. 'Do you not find it reassuring, Troy?'

Her pen hovered above a virgin page while Troy coped with the realisation of just how reassuring it was in fact. If Lucien had taken Angela Arturo to lunch it would have put her on at least the same footing as Troy, and the idea of his strolling along the waterfront with her as he had with Troy was something she did not even contemplate. As it was, there could have been no more time than it would take to drive there and back and make a few purchases.

'It doesn't make any difference to me,' she said carelessly. 'She wasn't going to be my aunt.'

'Hah!' He could sound very Italian at times, and she kept her eyes on the still empty page of her book while he snorted his disbelief. 'You would not have minded if he lunched with her?' he teased, looking upward into her face and smiling, watching the colour rise in her cheeks. 'You would have been quite happy to know that he was sitting in a restaurant with her, holding her hand?'

'Pietro! What Lucien does is none of my business, and if you don't keep quiet and let me get on I shall go back to the cottage!'

'Ah!'

'Oh, shut up!'

'O.K., O.K.!' He flung his cigarette away, then leaned back on his hands and was quiet for a few seconds before turning to look at her over his shoulder, a faint smile hovering on his mouth. 'Now you are angry with me, yes?' he guessed.

'I am angry with you, *no*!' Troy retorted. 'But I shall be if you don't give me five minutes' peace, Pietro!'

'O.K., O.K.!'

He subsided once more and Troy settled down to work yet again, transcribing her notes from one book to another, using her neatest handwriting instead of her normal hasty scribble, because she wanted no chance of mistakes when she came to type them out. The pile of small note-pads represented more than a month's work and it would be disastrous if she made a mistake—she might never get another change to do it again.

CHAPTER NINE

IT was not only the accuracy of her notes that made Troy
so preoccupied as she sat there with Pietro stretched out
beside her, but the fact that Lucien had been away such
a short time with Angela Arturo. It shouldn't concern
her, it *didn't* concern her, she told herself as she wrote
carefully and clearly, what Lucien did or with whom,
but nevertheless the thought of his returning so quickly
stayed in her mind and gave her a secret little glow of
pleasure whenever she dwelt on it.

The *mistral* blew briskly across the mountain face and
cooled the air, made it more bearable than the early
summer sun would have been, but it was some time
before she realised that there was some other smell than
the familiar scents of the maquis in the air. Looking up,
she sniffed, frowning slightly, then glanced down at
Pietro to see if he had noticed.

He lay flat on his back and appeared to be asleep so
that she hesitated to disturb him because he was less of a
distraction in his present state. The elusive smell still
reached her, however, and she looked in the other direction, down the hill towards the road. Immediately
around them the plants were low-growing, herbaceous
types with only an occasional shrub or tree standing up
among them, but lower down it grew higher. Dense
bushes of myrtle, gorse and broom formed thickets it
was sometimes hard to penetrate, and thick carpets of
bracken wrapped its fronds around their trunks.

It was from the more dense growth of maquis that she
suddenly recognised lazily spiralling plumes of yellow
smoke for what they were, with an occasional lick of
flame shooting upward from the heart of them. It must

have been going on for a while to have got such a hold, and she realised that if only she had not been so engrossed she would have noticed it before. She jerked into life suddenly and turned quickly to grab Pietro's arm, shaking him hard in case he was asleep.

'Pietro! Pietro, wake up quickly, there's a fire!'

He had spent enough time in Corsica among the mountains and forests to know what that could mean, but he was still boy enough to show fear in the first instance, and as he leapt to his feet his eyes were bright with the gleam of panic. *'Dio mio,'* he breathed, *'la sigaretta!'*

Troy had forgotten all about his carelessly disposed of cigarette end, but this was no time for recriminations. For even in those first few stunned seconds the flames overpowered the lazily spiralling smoke and leapt upwards, fanned by the freshness of the *mistral* and sweeping across the face of the mountain towards the vineyards. Troy's instinct was to run while there was still time to pass the ever-growing barrier that barred their way to the road, but Pietro had already rid himself of his first panic and his thought was for the vines.

Ripping off his shirt as he went, he chased down towards the spreading flames and began to beat at them with the improvised beater, but it was pitifully inadequate and he stood no chance of making any impression. Troy followed him instinctively, racing after him and not even noticing that her bag and notebooks still lay on the ground where they had fallen, her voice shrilly anxious as she called to him.

'Pietro, we have to get help, we can't do it alone, it's spreading too fast! We have to get help!'

He either did not hear or he chose to ignore her, for he still flapped at the flames ineffectually with his shirt, getting dangerously close in his determination, and Troy realised she would have to go herself if help was to be summoned. She veered off to the right because the fire was spreading rapidly to her left carried by the wind, but even while she was turning to go she saw something that brought her to an immediate halt, staring back along the edge of the fire.

'Pietro!'

He must have taken a careless step and overbalanced on the steep slope, for she saw him miss his footing and go rolling down into the fire while she watched in horrified helplessness. She scarcely believed her eyes when the impetus of his fall carried him on through the flames and beyond them, where he went sprawling among the taller scrub and lay still.

'Pietro!'

Her own cry came back to her faintly, but even before the echo had died she saw him move, pulling himself up from the ground and shaking his head; dirty and dazed but apparently unhurt. It was almost unbelievable, and yet she had seen it happen and her sigh of relief came from her lips like a prayer.

She found her legs alarmingly weak and unsteady as she turned to resume her own errand, and she choked on the drifting smoke as she cut in as close as she dared to save time. She would have to leave Pietro to cope as best he could until help came, but at least now she had the consolation of knowing that he was on the safe side of the fire and that it was blowing away from him.

It was something she should have remembered, that fire was a hazard constantly on anyone's mind who lived in such close proximity to the risk of it, and obviously the blaze had already been spotted from below. As she hurried down the slope she saw a group of men armed with beaters already climbing the hill and she slowed her pace to a standstill after a few more yards.

They were taking the path along the narrow clearing that bordered the vine fields, so that Troy was unobserved at first as she came from the opposite direction, but then she saw Pietro glance round, then hoist a reassuring thumb. Putting out the fire was the eventual aim, but keeping it away from the vines was the immediate objective and the men were working in from the far end, beating as they went and working against the wind, so far with gratifying success.

It was startling to realise what a weakening effect relief could have on her limbs, and Troy sank to the ground, rubbing a smoke-grimed arm across her hot forehead and thankful to leave everything in the hands of those much more experienced. She had been there for only a moment or two when shock brought her once more to her feet, her eyes blank with dismay.

All her notes, the sum total of her month's work, were still somewhere up there, lying on the ground exactly where she had dropped them in those first few stunned moments, and the flames were creeping nearer every minute, the fire-fighters concentrating on the other extremity of the blaze.

Impulse was always a moving factor with Troy, and she did not hesitate when she thought of all her work being consumed by fire; her painstaking research going up in smoke and leaving her the whole thing to do again—if it was ever possible. Her impulse sent her scrambling upwards once more, racing against the spread of the flames and panting for breath, choking when she got downwind of the smoke.

The wind shifted slightly and the area was wider now, so that she had to go wider round to get above it, but she had made up her mind and nothing would change it, not when her notes might still be intact up there. Coughing and shaking her head against the choking pall of smoke, she clambered past crackling gorse bushes and broom that flared like skeleton torches against a smoke-hazed sky, only to realise when she at last gained the far side that she could not remember exactly where she had been sitting.

It looked different, confusingly different, and the wind

gusted and smoke billowed over her, making her choke and stinging her eyes so that she turned away her head in an effort to escape it. There had been a tree, she remembered, a small eucalyptus and a gorse bush close by; if she could just identify them it was possible she would find her notes and get back past the fire again before it overtook her.

Wiping her streaming eyes with the back of her hand, she looked around her. It was near the spot, she felt sure; low-growing herbaceous plants above the line of taller shrubs; only so much of the taller vegetation had been burned that it was hard to recognise the original line. A solitary eucalyptus showed for a moment, fluttering its green leaves, then flared suddenly as if someone had put a match to it, and a nearby gorse bush sparked into flames, crackling and spitting, just in the moment she realised she had found it.

It was the same spot, but it was too late to do anything now, and the tears that streamed down her cheeks were not altogether brought on by the sting of smoke. She was no nearer to finishing her grandfather's book at this moment than she had been when she first set foot on Corsica, a month ago.

'Troy!' The cry, muffled by smoke and distance, reached her only faintly, but it served to snatch her back to consciousness, to an awareness of her danger. 'Troy, where are you?'

It was Pietro, she realised, anxious because he could no longer see her; he might even have seen her make her way back up the hill and had come looking for her. Turning quickly, she scrambled back down, making for the place where the wind laid the fire flat and swept it towards the men who were slowly but surely making headway in its destruction. It was as she spread her arms to balance herself and run down the increasing steepness of the slope that another call, another voice, reached her.

'Troy! Troy! *Dio mio*, will you answer me? Troy!'

'I'm coming!' She was hoarse, choked with smoke and tears, and obviously her call did not reach Lucien, although he was closer than Pietro had been.

'Troy! *Santa madre, aiutarmi, per favore!* Troy!'

The fervent prayer brought a jolt of urgency to her heart. It was Lucien at his most Italian, harshly passionate in his emotion and in the circumstances not likely to take kindly to the sight of her quite unharmed apart from stinging eyes and a grimy face. She saw him in the same instant he spotted her, rubbing a smoke-stained arm across his eyes as he looked around for her. Catching sight of her, he stared for a bare second, then came striding across, gripped her arm firmly and literally dragged her after him, past the blaze and down the hill.

'Lucien!'

She saw herself in danger of falling if she was made to go as fast when the ground was so uneven and her legs so tremblingly unsteady, but he stopped only when they were well clear of the fire. The hillside was scorched and blackened and the fire almost out, only an occasional fitful and defiant blaze, such as had consumed her notes with the surrounding trees, flaring up when the wind breathed new life into it.

But Troy noticed nothing of that; she was staring up into the dark stern face that glowered fiercely at her while strong fingers still gripped her wrist tight enough to hurt. His hands and arms were grimed and the smart slacks and shirt he had donned to take Signora Arturo shopping were rumpled and dirty, but it was the violence of emotion in his face that Troy gazed at in awe.

She was trembling and her legs felt barely able to support her, and she longed with an incredible longing to be wrapped in the comfort of his arms. It was a fact she recognised with resignation and made no attempt to understand, but Lucien was not offering comfort at the moment, he was far too angry. It had to be anger that made him look as he did; no other emotion could surely give him that gloweringly fierce look, or bring such glittering brightness to his black eyes.

'Go back with Pietro to the house!' he said in a voice that shook with the same emotion that glittered in his eyes, and she noticed how much more pronounced his accent was; how much more Italian he sounded when he was emotionally disturbed, as when she had heard him murmur that brief prayer up there.

'I'm all right,' she insisted in a small unsteady voice. 'I went to try and find my notes, but——'

'You risked your life for a notebook!' He cut her short, harshly derisive, and the hand that held her so tightly thrust away the arm he held so roughly that she flinched and soothed the marks of his fingers with her other hand. '*Dio mio*, how could anyone be so completely stupid!'

'They were important to me, Lucien!' She was too close to tears again and she did not want to cry; not with so many people around and Lucien looking as if he scarcely refrained from adding physical violence to verbal. 'They were all I had; my whole project has gone in a few minutes!'

'You count them more important than your life?' he asked, then seemed suddenly to notice the tears that streaked through the grime on her face. '*Piccola idiota!*' he said, shaking his head, and reached out to pull her into his arms, holding her close while his face rested on her hair that smelled of smoke and burned brushwood, and it no longer seemed to matter that there were other people about.

He was right to call her a little fool, because she had acted impulsively rather than sensibly, and she pressed her face close to the smoky damp softness of his shirt beneath which a broad tanned chest pulsed with a throbbing beat close to her ear.

'I'm a fool,' she allowed, and clung more tightly still

when he laughed.

'And honest too,' he said.

It was quite clear that Pietro felt deeply about his responsibility for her loss and he was unusually quiet and subdued as they made their way back to the house, but Troy was still a little too dazed at the moment to lay the blame anywhere. He walked right around to the cottage with her to her front door, and it was when he was on the point of leaving that she raised the subject that must be on both their minds.

'Don't look so down in the mouth, Pietro,' she told him. 'I'm not blaming you.'

'You *should*—I blame myself!' His mask of tragedy reminded her once more of that Corsican taste for drama. 'If I had not been so careless you would not have to begin your work all over again! You should hate me!'

Troy ignored the dramatics, but shook her head over the question of beginning again. 'I'm not sure I shall do it all over again, Pietro,' she said, and realised he was staring at her and frowning. It had probably not even occurred to him that she might lack the heart to start all over again, or that she might not have the chance to remain in the cottage, and looking up at him she smiled ruefully. 'It isn't a five-minute job, you know,' she reminded him, 'and I can't really expect Lucien to go on being my landlord indefinitely.'

'Oh, but you must, Troy!' He took her hands and stood holding them so tightly that there was no chance of her doing anything about it at the moment. 'I could not bear it if your grandfather's book was not completed because of me! And Lucien will never speak to me again if you go away so disappointed!'

Troy did not speculate on Lucien's reaction at the moment, but shook her head and gently eased her hands free, spreading them wide in a gesture she found herself using with increasing frequency lately. 'I'll have to see how things work out,' she told him. 'I just haven't the heart to even think about it at the moment.'

'But you will not pack up and go home without thinking very hard?' Pietro begged, his eyes darkly appealing. 'Please promise that you will not do that, Troy!'

It was not a difficult promise to make, although she had no way of knowing how possible it would be to keep, so she nodded and smiled as she looked up at him. 'Very well,' she agreed, 'I'll give it a couple of days anyway, and see how I feel—and how Lucien feels about me keeping the cottage.'

'He will agree,' Pietro assured her confidently. 'I know he will!'

'Let's hope so.' She looked down at her grubby dress and hands and pulled a face. 'Now I'd better go and do something about making myself more presentable, Pietro, and so had you.'

'You cannot go away until you have told me what you think I should do,' Pietro reminded her, apparently heedless of any need to do as she suggested, and Troy shook her head over the problem that it seemed was never allowed to rest for very long.

'I wish you'd make up your own mind about that, Pietro; I'd much rather you did.'

She felt dirty and uncomfortable, and she wished he did too and then perhaps he would do something about it, but instead he simply stood there beside the door with one hand on the frame and avoiding her eyes as he usually did whenever they discussed his determined stand against his father. There was a certain stubborn look about his mouth and jaw that reminded her inescapably of his uncle, and it brought to her a sudden and unexpected feeling of tenderness when she recognised it, although she could not think why it should.

'Look, I feel horribly grubby at the moment,' she

pleaded. 'Let's leave that until another time, shall we, Pietro?'

'But you will stay?' She looked up at him, but before she could reply he made his own point. 'I shall speak to Lucien,' he said firmly, '*he* will make you stay!'

Troy put a hand on the door handle and pushed the door open, smiling at him briefly over her shoulder. 'We'll see,' she promised. 'Now for heaven's sake go and clean up before your mother sees you!'

He grinned, a confident gesture that beamed whitely in his grimy features. 'O.K.,' he agreed, and waved a hand as he turned to go. *'Ciao, bella mia!'*

Smiling and shaking her head at such irrepressible confidence, Troy went in for a bath, a long hot soak in scented water that dispelled the stench of burned brushwood and restored the glowing freshness to her skin. Her hair she shampooed twice over, then towelled it dry in the sun through the window, until it looked its usual glossy red-brown.

A clean fresh loose cotton dress completed her transformation and she felt a different person as she prepared herself a light midday meal. Since the first gift, Lucien had brought over another two bottles of his best wine and she finished off the first of those with her meal, feeling a sense of well-being as she cleared the table afterwards. There was no reason why she should not begin again, as Pietro said, if Lucien was willing to let her stay on, and she did not really doubt that he would be.

The front windows of the cottage faced across the yard that divided it from the house, and from her *salon* window it was possible to see one of the windows of the room she knew to be Lucien's office. Not that she ever deliberately looked across there, for she had no wish for her host to think he was observed, but sometimes she caught a glimpse of someone over there, usually Lucien himself or one of the estate workers, and her attention was attracted without her being entirely conscious of it.

That was how it was now. A slight movement opposite and it was automatic to glance across before turning away again. There were two figures in this instance, and Troy turned her head away even more quickly than usual when she recognised them. Not only because of who they were but because of what they were doing.

There could be no mistaking Lucien, tall and lean and dark as a brigand with his ruggedly sensual face and black-eyed, and nor was it difficult to recognise his companion. The only blonde head she had seen about La Casa Antica was Angela Arturo, and at the moment that same blonde head was tilted backwards while she wrapped her arms around Lucien's neck and raised her red mouth to his kiss.

It shouldn't hurt, and Troy did her best not to let it, but there seemed nothing she could do about the sharp thudding beat of her heart as she turned away and walked on legs that were not quite steady to the other side of the little room. It wasn't possible to get very far away from the scene in the house opposite, but she got as far away as she could, looking out of the far window at the pale green vines strung out on the hillside.

It should not surprise her either, for Angela Arturo's feelings were blatantly obvious, and heaven knew Lucien had made enough allusions to his other guest to leave little doubt how the land lay as far as he was concerned, no matter what Bianca said. The fact that he had been so readily willing to console Troy after losing his temper with her for taking chances was neither here nor there. He was an emotionally passionate man and her foolish action had aroused his fears, as it would have whoever she had been.

So she told herself over and over while she stared out unseeingly. Lucien had boasted that he could handle the blonde woman easily enough; or if he had not used those exact words the implication had been the same, and he had never pretended to dislike her sex. Given the kind of encouragement that Angela Arturo offered, there was no reason for him to resist; she would have been surprised if he had.

What puzzled Troy most was her own reaction to it, and she gave a few moments' thought to it while she made up her mind what to do with herself now that she no longer had her notes to occupy her time. She liked Lucien—no, that was not the right word to use in connection with a man like Lucien Gaffori; he aroused much deeper reactions than that and she was no less a woman than Angela Arturo. She——

'Troy?'

That soft lingering echo after her name sent a shivering little thrill of response through her body as she turned quickly to the half-open door. His shadow fell darkly across the light wall and she had the brief impression that it looked sinister, then immediately dismissed it as fanciful. Shaking herself back to normality, she called out to him.

'Yes, Lucien, come in!'

A clean white shirt and light slacks replaced the grimy clothes she had last seen him wearing, and she despaired once more of her own response to him as he stood for a moment in the doorway. A hand ran its fingers through sable-dark hair and he ducked his head slightly because the lintel was rather low, black eyes gleaming at her confidently as he came into the little *salon*. A long and boldly explicit gaze noted the improvements she had made since their last encounter, and he smiled.

'I am glad to see you are no worse for your experience,' he said. 'I do not think I asked if you had been hurt, and that was very remiss of me. Please forgive me.'

Troy steadied her voice determinedly and shook her head over the belated enquiry. 'I'm perfectly all right,' she told him, and glanced quite instinctively down at the wrist she imagined could still feel the strength of his fingers. 'The only bruises I'm likely to have are from you grabbing me so hard!'

A black brow flicked upward briefly and she was sure she did not imagine the slight narrowing of his eyes for a moment. 'I am sorry for that also, but you must allow that I had cause for anger.'

Sorry now that she had even mentioned it, Troy nodded, her own fingers encircling her wrist in a quite unconscious imitation of his. 'Yes, of course you did. I wasn't complaining, Lucien.' Seeking safer ground than her impulsive foolishness, she remembered that the fire had still been smouldering when she and Pietro left the scene. 'Is everything under control now?'

Lucien shrugged and she thought he sensed something in her manner, although she did her best to appear normal. If only the memory of him standing there in the window and kissing Angela Arturo did not disturb her so, but she could not get it out of her mind. It still affected her when she recalled those slim arms wound about his neck and the red mouth upturned to his kiss, and the fact that she was so affected troubled her almost as much as the incident itself.

Without waiting for an invitation to sit down he perched himself on the edge of the marble-topped table as Pietro did so often when he came to see her, regarding her for a moment without saying anything. 'Fire is something we learn to deal with here,' he said after a while. 'Fortunately one of the men saw it start and called for help or it could have been disastrous with everything so dry, both for you and Pietro and the crop.'

'Yes. Yes, I realise that and I'm grateful you came and fetched me back, Lucien. I hadn't realised how silly it was to go back to try and find my notes, but I was so— appalled to think of them going up in smoke I simply didn't stop to think.'

'Impulsive, yes?' His voice was gentle, persuasive, and Troy began to sense something of his purpose suddenly; her heart thudding anxiously when his next question confirmed it. 'You do not smoke, do you, Troy?'

'No.' She did not want to answer him and she moved away towards the window to try and evade those steady black eyes that watched her. 'No, I don't.'

'Pietro does—on occasion.'

She remembered how Pietro not only smoked the same cigarettes as his uncle but also copied his gestures so faithfully too, and she felt bound to defend him. Turning round to look at him, she tried to conceal her eyes with half-lowered lids. 'He tries to be like you,' she said, and did not quite manage to keep the hint of appeal out of her voice. 'He smokes the same brand of cigarettes and he copies your gestures, your—mannerisms. I noticed that!'

For a moment the black eyes held hers steadily and she saw a sudden warmth in them that she could not immediately find a reason for until he answered her. 'So you observe my gestures and mannerisms so closely that you can identify them in my nephew, is that what you are telling me, Troy?'

Somehow that soft deep voice had always affected her more than she cared to admit, and Troy shook her head to deny the intimacy it suggested. 'I'm just trying to say that he wants to be like you, Lucien, in every way. He admires you, tries to copy you, and he's very young, he doesn't always stop to think.'

'Is that also your reason for acting impulsively, *cara mia*?' he asked softly, and smiled. 'You are very little older than Pietro, are you?'

Her cheeks flushed a warm pink and her eyes brightly blue, Troy fought hard to restrain her suddenly rising temper. 'I'm simply trying to explain that Pietro isn't a vandal simply because he caused that fire, Lucien,' she told him breathlessly, 'that's all! My age doesn't come into it, but since you've raised the subject, I'm certainly not a schoolgirl, even though you seem to think I am, judging by the way you're talking at the moment!'

He did not move for a moment, but held her unwilling gaze until she turned away, unable to account for the sudden fury of emotion that burned in her. Then she heard the slight swish when he slid off the surface of the marble table and her body tensed, waiting for him to touch her as she knew he would.

His hands were laid on her arms, long strong fingers turning her slowly to face him, then drawing her close to the inflexible leanness of his body until she was pressed close and her heart almost stopped in the excitement of it. He wound his arms about her, one hand cradling the back of her head so that her face was tipped up to him, her mouth parted and waiting for his kiss.

Bending his head, he murmured something in Italian that the drumming beat of her heart almost overwhelmed, then his lips touched hers, just a light gentle touch that promised so much more. Her eyes half-closed, her body turned in his arms as she reached up to put her arms about his neck, and from below the thick shadow of her lashes she caught a glimpse of the window opposite—the window of Lucien's office.

So swiftly that she took him by surprise, she dropped her arms and put her hands against his chest, using all her force to break his hold on her. For just a second or two he held her, even against her determined struggles his arms refused to yield, and then suddenly he let her break away and she went quickly across the room and stood with her back to him.

The little room was silent and she could almost swear she heard his breathing, except that her own breathing was so short and uneven that it made all other sounds uncertain. She dared not even glance over her shoulder to make sure that he was still there, but that was soon determined when he spoke, softly and without moving from the spot.

'I was perhaps more accurate than you allowed, *carissima mia*, hmm? I am sorry if I alarmed you, that was

not my intention, you must know that.' A deep snatch of
laughter caught at her senses for a second. 'I have to
confess to misjudgment, and you cannot know what that
does to my pride!'

Troy wanted to say so much; to deny that he had
misjudged her initial willingness to be kissed, but when
she turned to look at him the black eyes were watching
her with such intensity that the words died on her lips
and she simply shook her head. He studied her for a
moment as if he still needed to be convinced of his misjudgment, then he smiled wryly and thrust both hands
into his pockets.

'I will promise not to say anything of Pietro's part in
the fire,' he said, as if he had found a possible solution.
'Will that make you happier, Troy?'

The lingering echo after her name sent her pulses
racing and she nodded without looking up at him. He
moved quietly for a big man and she did not realise he
had come across to her until she felt the warmth of his
nearness and instinctively turned towards him. A big
hand lifted her chin and he gazed down into her face for
a moment without speaking.

'I would like to understand you, *piccola mia*,' he said
softly, then once again gave that short snatch of laughter
and shook his head, letting his hand slide from beneath
her chin. 'Perhaps one day, hah?'

CHAPTER TEN

IT was Madame Coron who informed Troy of the latest turn of events the following day. Signor Gerolamo had ordered his wife to return to Rome without delay, and Pietro was to come with her. Obviously the Signor had decided that his wife had been absent from the family home long enough and was taking steps to bring matters to a head, as Bianca had forecast he would.

So far Pietro himself had said nothing about it, for the simple reason that Troy had taken care to avoid him since she found out. A man authoritative enough to *order* his wife home, as Madame Coron claimed, was not going to accept the ruling of a complete stranger with regard to the career of his elder son, and particularly when she was very little older than the son herself—a fact that Lucien had gone to the trouble of pointing out yesterday.

It was with the idea of remaining uncommitted for as long as possible that Troy took herself off immediately after breakfast and drove into Dentreau without saying a word to anyone. She lunched there and took care to make sure the coast was clear before she drove up to the house on her return.

It was mid-afternoon when she set off for her favourite place, up on the mountainside, and the Vincentello children joined her just before she reached the terraces. The way through the vines was shorter and she had used it ever since Pietro pointed out the advantages of it, even though it meant taking a chance on seeing Lucien.

The sun was warm and she could anticipate the cooler breeze higher up with pleasure as the children chattered away alongside her. They knew how sparse her French was, but they had such touching faith in her ability to understand them that she actually found herself making the effort, something she had not bothered about too much before.

It was little Marie, tiny and doll-like, who spotted Lucien at the far end of one of the rows of vines as they passed, and waved a hand to attract his attention. Lucien was a special favourite of Marie's, and Troy was forced to acknowledge the fact that he was capable of attracting females of all ages.

Her own reaction to him was less voluble than the little girl's but scarcely less excited, although she did her best to appear cool and calm. It was not easy to forget that brief moment in her cottage yesterday when, against instinct, she had rejected his kiss because she had caught sight of the window where she had seen him kissing Angela Arturo only a very short time before.

He looked much as he had the very first time she saw him, in dark cord trousers held by a silver-buckled belt, a collarless shirt and that raffish kerchief knotted around his brown throat. Earthy and undeniably sensual and, she was forced to admit, the most exciting man she had ever seen. Seeing them, he hesitated briefly, then came striding towards them between the rows of vines, and Troy watched him come with mixed feelings.

'Troy—hello!'

He curled his long fingers around Marie's tiny hand but spared the children only a brief glance, and when he smiled Troy felt it was a slightly more reserved smile than usual. She wondered if it was possible that he felt slightly self-conscious after yesterday's incident, but almost immediately dismissed the idea as unlikely. Not to be outdone, she smiled too, and even more certainly.

'Hello, Lucien.'

He hesitated for a moment, then looked down at the children and his black eyes warmed when he looked at little Marie. It was instinctive, Troy guessed, for he liked children and his response to them was automatic. Then bending his tall figure over he spoke to them, addressing himself primarily to the little girl, kissing her baby cheek lightly and taking her hand in his while he spoke quietly in French.

Marie's dark eyes turned curiously to Troy and for a moment she frowned, then her brother nudged her and she nodded. *'Oui, monsieur.'*

'Jérome?' He prompted the boy and Jérome smiled and nodded.

'Mais oui, Monsieur Gaffori!'

Coins were handed over and two small hands clasped them eagerly, withdrawn from hers while they gloated over their newly acquired riches. Obviously they were much more interested in having money to spend and had been given it presumably as a persuasion to leave her, but Troy blinked a little uncertainly as she watched them go scampering off, waving their hands and calling as they ran.

'Au revoir, monsieur; au revoir, mademoiselle—merci, merci!'

When they were out of earshot Lucien turned back to her, black eyes speculating as he studied her for a moment before he said anything. 'You do not mind?' he asked, and Troy barely moved her head.

'Why did you do that, Lucien?'

'Give them money to spend?' He was being deliberately evasive, she knew, but there was something very different about him today that she could not quite fathom out. 'I have done so before, Troy—their father does not object, although he tells me that I spoil them. But they are enchanting, are they not? Especially *la petite* Marie!' His eyes drew hers and held them steadily and his voice had that soft, deep sound that Troy always found so disturbing. 'Maybe I should have a family of my own, eh, *mia cara*?'

Troy could find no answer to that, for it was something she was wondering about herself. He thrust both hands into the front pockets of his trousers and regarded her for a moment in silence, and it was only when she found the silence too discomfiting and raised her eyes that she realised he was smiling. Not with his mouth, although that twitched suspiciously at its corners, but in the deep glittering blackness of his eyes.

'I wished to tell you, *mia piccola*,' he said as soon as she looked at him, 'that Pietro's *papa* has—ordered that he be brought home by his mother. I thought that you should know.'

Troy shook her head, too uneasy to think clearly. 'I know,' she confessed. 'Madame Coron told me this morning when I went over to the house to fetch my breakfast rolls.'

'Ah, of course! Madame Coron is devoted to Pietro and thinks that he should not be made to do things he does not wish.' The smile became more evident and he shook his head. 'He has the gift of making women feel for him, that one, eh?'

'You, of all people, surely can't be surprised at *that*!' Troy retorted swiftly, and Lucien laughed.

'I am not surprised, *mia piccola,* merely remarking on a fact. Another fact, however, is that the time has come when you can no longer avoid giving him your answer, and I know that it will be the *right* answer, eh, Troy?'

He was so sure she would do as he wanted her to, it was clearly written there on that dark confident face. She knew his feelings in the matter and it would not even cross his mind that she would do other. Into her mind came the image of him standing in the window of his office with Angela Arturo's arms twined around his neck and her mouth lifted up to his, and Troy swallowed hard on the violent reaction it aroused in her still. She seemed unable to rid herself of that image.

'Troy?'

For a second that lingering ghost of an 'a' almost made her forget again, but she angled her chin and

summoned every ounce of composure she possessed.
'Yes, I know the right answer,' she said, and was appalled to realise how tempted she was to tell Pietro her
answer was the opposite to what he expected, simply for
the sake of taking that blandly confident look off Lucien's face.

'Have you told Pietro yet?'

Troy half-turned, presenting a shoulder to him instead
of facing him because she could not forget either that
facing him it was so easy to be drawn into his arms.
'No—no, I haven't. I'll tell him later.'

It must have been something in her face; perhaps that
half-formed temptation to advise Pietro against defying
his father showed briefly in her manner, for she sensed
the stiffening of Lucien's panther-lean body, a sudden
tension that affected her own nerves as well. A brief
glance at his face showed a frown drawing black brows
close above glittering eyes, and the muscles in his bare
arms were taut under the tanned skin. He had read something into her hesitant answer that was never intended,
but before she could tell him so he forestalled her.

'Troy, I cannot believe it! You could not disappoint
him—you could not disappoint *me* like that! *Dio mio*,
how can you be so heartless!'

If she imagined his mouth kissing Angela Arturo's
bright lips it was easy to admit that she might momentarily have taken pleasure in hurting him, but the fact
that he so quickly judged her heartless was something she
found hard to accept, and when she looked up at him her
blue eyes had the brightness of tears as well as anger.

'What makes you most angry, Lucien?' she asked in a
voice that shivered unsteadily. 'The fact that I'd disappoint Pietro, or that you can't believe I'd do other than
what *you* want me to?'

She turned swiftly away from the look that hovered
behind the anger in his eyes. 'I am angry because I
thought you had compassion and I do not like to be so

wrong about anyone, and particularly not about you, Troy! I had not imagined you as cruel!'

Troy snatched at her anger desperately and clung to it, for a touch of his hand, she believed, would be enough to break her resistance, and she had the wildest idea that behind his anger there was the same desire that had made him kiss her yesterday. She could not pretend not to want his kisses, but she hated the idea of sharing them with Angela Arturo.

'Why, when you have nothing to lose,' Lucien demanded in harsh exasperation, 'must you let Pietro down?'

'I'm not!'

She was too late to avoid the hands that reached out and gripped her arms with bruising strength, bringing her round to face him, but she turned her head away. Immediately hard fingers held her chin and forced her to look up. 'Or is it me that you wish to—get at, Troy?' he demanded.

Her heart was thudding wildly and her legs felt scarcely capable of supporting her, and yet it was not fear of him that weakened her so, she knew. His temper was harsh and violent but he would not harm her, she felt sure of it, not really hurt her. His hold on her simply ensured that she did not evade him and he held her chin only hard enough to make sure she did not look away. His emotions were fierce and turbulent, but she had no fear of him.

'Let me go, please, Lucien!'

He studied her face closely and while he did so his hold relaxed just a fraction. It was all Troy needed, and she turned quickly, evading his hands, and ran along the row of vines as fast as she could towards the thick, all-concealing maquis where she could hide, for a while at least.

He would know how wrong he was about her decision soon enough, but in the meantime she had a great deal of thinking to do about her own situation. She didn't want to fall in love with Lucien; it was about the most foolish thing she could do, but at the moment she could see little hope of undoing what was already a painful fact.

It was late before Troy returned to the cottage, and the field workers were going home for the day. One man only lingered, completing some task he preferred not to leave, but there was no sign of Lucien, and she breathed a sigh of relief. It was close on time for dinner, of course, so he was most likely gone home as the men had done, in time for the evening meal.

The cottage seemed strangely empty and lonely when she let herself in, and she found she had little appetite, although the second bottle of wine that Lucien had given her did something to console her. If she felt no better about things tomorrow, she would seriously think about going home, no matter what transpired in the Gerolamo family.

The effect of three glasses of wine with a much smaller meal than usual was pleasantly soporific, and she was still sitting at the table when someone knocked on the door. Immediately all traces of sleepiness vanished and she sat upright on her chair, staring at the closed door and pressing a hand to the thudding beat of her heart.

'Troy!'

No one else ever achieved quite the same effect with that extra syllable, and she got up only slowly from the table watching the door as she walked across the room. Apparently she was too slow in answering, for she was no more than half way across the room when the door opened and Lucien stood in the doorway.

He hesitated for a second when he saw her, then glanced across at the window facing out across the yard. Very deliberately he switched on the light beside the door, then came across and took her arm, taking her across to the window. He looked across at his office window and then back to her, and Troy knew he had somehow discovered that she had witnessed his interlude with Angela Arturo.

She would have spoken, protested that she had not invited him in and that he had no right to act as if he owned her as well as the cottage, but Lucien pulled her into his arms, giving her no chance to resist, and found her mouth unerringly. His kiss was hard and relentless and he held her so tightly that her head spun as the breath was crushed out of her. She was scarcely able to stand when he at last raised his head and looked down into her face with gleaming black eyes that dismissed any chance of there being an apology this time.

'Perhaps someone has seen me kiss *you*,' he said in a voice that she noticed was not quite steady, even in her present state. 'Do you care, *carissima mia*?'

Breathless and momentarily stunned, Troy could only shake her head, but when the dark face loomed nearer again and the warmth of his breath was on her lips, she struggled for a moment against the fierce strength of his arms, shaking her head urgently. 'No, Lucien!'

'You saw me with Angela, *sí*?' he demanded, and made nonsense of her efforts to be free of him, his arms held her as tightly as ever and he was smiling, that stunningly wolfish smile she remembered uneasily from their first encounter. 'Is that what made you reject me so determinedly yesterday, Troy? Is it?'

'I saw you,' Troy answered, whispering because she had not breath enough to speak any more forcefully, and she once more struggled in his arms. 'I couldn't help seeing you, but I could do something about being next on your list, Lucien! Let me go, please, I——'

'Don't want me to kiss you?' The black eyes glittered confidently and his arms relaxed not one inch but pressed her as hard as ever to the fiercely possessive hardness of him. 'Now you will listen to me, *piccina*, while I tell you the truth about Angela Arturo and a lot of other things. You will listen, eh?'

'I don't——'

His mouth silenced her with a determination there was no hope of resisting, and she nodded wordlessly when she at last yielded to the inevitable and stood close in the circle of his arms while he talked. His deep, soft voice slightly muffled by the thickness of her hair, one hand stroking lightly over its silky smoothness.

'You saw Angela kiss me? Yes, yes, that is right, *piccola*,' he insisted hastily, and pressed his mouth to her neck as if to convince her. 'She is a very determined woman and not unattractive.' Troy raised her head and he kissed the soft reproachful lips before he smiled. 'I had not anticipated being seen, *carissima*, and especially not by you. I could not believe that you were rejecting me so harshly because you dislike me so much.' His conceit had the same unabashed frankness as Pietro's and she found herself smiling when he buried his face in the softness of her hair for a moment.

'You had no alternative but to kiss her, of course?' she whispered, and he eased her away from him for long enough to frown at her in mock severity.

'It is not very gallant to fight off a lady with kissing on her mind, *bella mia*, although if you had stayed for long enough at your window you would have observed that I released myself with as much swiftness as you did from the same situation yesterday!' A large brown hand smoothed the hair from her brow and the look in his black eyes sent shivering little thrills through her body. 'Will you believe that I would have done anything rather than have you witness that moment, Troy, however innocent it was?'

'Because I want to believe it,' Troy said, and laughed shakily because she could not yet quite believe this was happening. 'What made you come here now—right this minute?' she asked, and Lucien cupped her face in his hands, looking down at her for a long moment without speaking.

'Because I could not bear to remember you running away from me as you did this afternoon, *diletta mia*. I did not want to believe that you were going to behave so cruelly to Pietro because of something I had unwittingly done to anger you. It was when I stood at the window over there that I realised how easy it was to see from one room to the other, and I remembered.'

Troy looked down at her hands, curled loosely against his chest, and then glanced up briefly into his face, her eyes as irresistibly appealing as Pietro's sometimes were. 'Do you really believe I'm cruel, Lucien? Do you honestly believe I'd take a different decision because I saw you kiss Angela Arturo?'

'Because you saw Angela kiss *me, carissima*!' He looked down at her with such gentleness in his eyes that she knew she could never love anyone else, even if he had been the one doing the kissing. 'I do not know what I believed, *amore mia*; I perhaps got the wrong end of another stick, eh?' He bent his head and kissed her lingeringly, holding her close with his big gentle hands, soothingly persuasive. 'I knew that I loved you, my Troy, and I wanted you more than I have wanted anything in my life. Will you believe that? Please believe it, my love; I want to marry you.'

'Lucien.' She raised her face to him, her lips parted, wanting his kiss and responding to the wild incredible emotions that filled her with a longing she could not resist. 'I love you, I think——' She laughed breathlessly and reached up to put her arms around her neck. Once again, just as it had been the last time she did the same thing, she caught sight of the window opposite as she turned in his arms, but this time she did not push him away, she lifted her mouth to his kiss. 'I think I've always loved you,' she said, and believed she meant it.

It was several minutes before she remembered anything about Pietro and the need to tell him her answer, and by then she realised that her position as unbiassed adviser had changed somewhat in the past few minutes. Leaning back in Lucien's arms, she looked up into that dark, brigand's face with a smile that made him bend his head and kiss her throat while he murmured softly in Italian.

'Lucien, how can I be said to be a detached judge of what Pietro should do when——' She tiptoed and kissed his lips. 'I'm no longer in a position to say anything, my darling, am I?'

'Because you will be my wife?' She savoured that for a moment and nodded smilingly, then Lucien's arms tightened around her once more and she was pulled close into his arms, pressed to the virile leanness of him while he cradled her head to the strong beat of his heart. 'Pietro will stand his ground, *amante*, if there are enough of us to support him, and Bianca will do as much as she can, which will be enough, I think. I know how much Pietro, her husband, loves her.'

Holding tightly to him, Troy pressed her hands to the broad back and looked up into his face. It was hard to think about anything but Lucien at the moment, but she owed it to Pietro to at least think about his problem, and she gave her attention for the moment. 'You think Bianca can influence him?' she asked, and Lucien laughed softly and kissed her brow.

'Bianca has found a new strength from somewhere,' he told her. 'I think perhaps the happiness of her firstborn has aroused her to a sense of her own power.' Seeing her slight frown, he laughed and kissed her again. 'Bianca is a beautiful woman with an adoring husband who must have been missing her very much,' he explained. 'There is a great deal such a woman may achieve if she realises her own power. He adores her and she can twist him around her little finger. That is right, yes?' Troy nodded, smiling.

'And you've been putting ideas into her head?' she guessed.

Lucien's black eyes gleamed between their thick lashes and he bent his head once more to bring his mouth close to hers. 'You will do the same thing with me many times, I am quite certain,' he whispered, and parted her lips with his, kissing her lightly and teasingly until she closed her eyes. 'I love you, *amante*, and I wish to talk only of you, to show you how much I love you. Troy, *mia bella* Troy. *Ti amo, carissima mia!*'

Lifting her mouth to him, Troy willingly complied. She had no wish to think or talk about anyone else except the two of them, and when Lucien bent his head to kiss her, the only other thing she was conscious of was the sweet lingering scent of the maquis that drifted in through the open windows.

And there's still *more* love in

Harlequin Presents...

Do you have a favorite
Harlequin author?
Then here is an
opportunity you must
not miss!

HARLEQUIN OMNIBUS

Each volume contains
3 full-length compelling
romances by one author.
Almost 600 pages of
the very best in romantic
fiction for only $2.75

A wonderful way to collect
the novels by the Harlequin
writers you love best!